What if...
You Broke All the Rules

Check out all the
What if books!

What if . . . Everyone Knew Your Name

What if . . . All the Boys Wanted You

And coming in fall 2007:

What if . . . Everyone Was Doing It

a choose
your destiny
NOVEL

What if...
You Broke All the Rules

LIZ RUCKDESCHEL AND SARA JAMES

DELACORTE PRESS

Published by Delacorte Press
an imprint of Random House Children's Books
a division of Random House, Inc.
New York

www.randomhouse.com/teens
www.thewhatifbooks.com

Educators and librarians, for a variety of teaching tools, visit us at
www.randomhouse.com/teachers

Library of Congress Cataloging-in-Publication Data
Ruckdeschel, Liz.
What if— you broke all the rules? : a choose your destiny
novel / by Liz Ruckdeschel and Sara James. — 1st ed.
p. cm.
Summary: Armed with a new camcorder, Haley continues her
sophomore year at Hillsdale High, as the reader's choices help
her navigate a series of events that begin with a potentially
disastrous New Year's Eve party and end with what
could be the spring break of her dreams.
ISBN-13: 978-0-385-73501-8 (trade) ISBN-13: 978-0-385-90495-7
(lib. bdg.)
1. Plot-your-own stories. [1. Friendship—Fiction. 2. Video
recording—Fiction. 3. High schools—Fiction. 4. Schools—Fiction.
5. Plot-your-own stories.] I. James, Sara. II. Title.
PZ7.R842Whg 2007
[Fic]—dc22
2007002411

The text of this book is set in 12.5-point Apollo MT.

Printed in the United States of America

10 9 8 7 6 5 4

First Edition

What if...
You Broke All the Rules

In the Miller household,
it's definitely better to
give than to receive.

"Well, what is it?" Joan asked expectantly.

Haley looked down at the now unwrapped package in her lap and cringed.

"Come on, Haley, show us what Grandma Polly gave you this year," Haley's rumpled dad said from behind his digital video camera. Perry next panned over for a shot of Haley's plump, gray-haired grandmother sitting next to the Christmas tree, busily exercising her knitting needles. "I bet it's something grrrreat," he added. "Gam Polly always gives the kids the best presents. Don't you, Ma?"

"Oh, Perry," Haley's grandmother said, dismissing her son with a wave of her hand.

Yeah, right, Haley thought, *like that bright yellow owl sweater-vest with the googly eyes? Awesome.*

No matter how hard Haley had tried to get rid of the babyish sweater-vest that had been sitting in her closet for years, her parents were bent on keeping it. "For posterity," they said. But Haley knew it wasn't just for posterity. Whenever Gam Polly came to visit, Joan and Perry made Haley wear it, to breakfast, to lunch, to school, to dinner with friends. Just thinking about it made her itch.

"I hope you like it, dear," Gam said, stitching away.

Haley looked at her grandmother's latest project and felt momentarily sorry for whichever family member was destined to receive it. The yarn piled high in Gam's lap was rainbow-hued and sparkly. Haley shuddered. After years of being on the receiving end of such wacky, homespun gifts, she now saw those knitting needles for what they really were: weapons of mass humiliation.

"I'm sure she'll love it," said Perry, still filming. "Haley loves *everything* you make her. Don't you, sweetie?"

Haley looked down at the package in her lap. *Love* was definitely not the word that was coming to mind.

"Come on, Haley," Joan said, prodding. "Mitchell wants to open his presents too."

"When is. My turn," Haley's little brother asked impatiently in his signature robot voice.

"Soon, baby," Joan cooed.

Since she could put it off no longer, Haley finally lifted the garment out of its box. "It's a, um . . . It's a panda bear dress," she said, forcing a smile and unfurling the knitted dress for all to see. Three pandas lined the front, and Haley now noticed that their fluffy tails all poked out the back.

Of course, she thought. *There's no way one side of this thing would actually be wearable.*

"Isn't that just the cutest thing you've ever seen?" Perry marveled. "Mom, you've really outdone yourself this year."

"It looks. Like roadkill," Mitchell said mechanically. Haley's mother cupped her hand over his mouth to shush him, while Haley stifled a giggle. Normally, she found Mitchell's robot talk annoying. But today she agreed with him one hundred percent.

"That's Haley's Christmas sweater, buddy," Perry said, patting Mitchell on the head. "Isn't it cool? I bet you've got something just like it waiting for you in your box."

"One can only hope," Joan said under her breath.

"Well, Haley. Aren't you going to put it on?" her dad asked.

Haley shot her mother a desperate look. *Please don't make me wear it,* her eyes pleaded. *I'm too old to be seen in something that has a face and paws.*

"Does she really have to put it on, Perry?" Joan

said, looking sympathetically at her daughter. "Can't we at least wait till later? After we've opened all the other presents?"

"But we need to capture this moment on film," Perry replied.

"I would like to see how it fits," Gam added, glancing over the rims of her spectacles.

Haley knew in that instant that she was done for. Joan Miller might be able to tackle the biggest corporate polluters in the state of New Jersey at her law office, but when it came to standing up to her mother-in-law, Haley's mom was a complete and total wimp.

"She's probably right," Joan said, caving. "We should see if it fits. You have . . . developed quite a lot since the last time Gam saw you."

Haley's face flushed. She knew her mom was only trying to politely point out to Gam that her little granddaughter was growing up. But still, why did parents always have to use the word *developed* when they were really talking about boobs?

Haley grabbed the sweater and marched off to the powder room to slip it on. *Maybe it'll be too small,* she hoped, pulling the door closed behind her. Off came her pajamas. She held up the sweaterdress, stuck her tongue out at the pandas, and tugged it down over her newfound curves.

Unfortunately, the dress not only fit, it was comfortable without being baggy, snug without being too tight. In fact, if it weren't for the pandas, Haley thought, looking down at her figure, it might actually have been sort of cute.

That was the unfortunate thing about Gam's signature knitwear: it could expand and contract to fit almost anyone. Which meant it was virtually impossible to outgrow. At least in the physical sense.

"You look . . . darling," her grandmother said, admiring her own handiwork after Haley emerged from the bathroom. "Just darling."

"Joanie, get the thirty-five-millimeter," Perry said from behind the camcorder. "I want to take next year's Christmas card shot as soon as Mitchell opens his gift."

"Uh!" Gam exclaimed. "Won't that be sweet!"

Haley was about to protest when she heard the doorbell ring. *Whew,* she thought, *saved by the bell.* "I'll get it," she offered, hoping to stall the inevitable embarrassment of having her picture taken. The last thing she wanted was a framed photo of the panda fiasco hanging on the living room wall, or worse, sent out to a few hundred of the Millers' closest friends. *That would be unthinkable,* she thought as she answered the door.

Oh, but the embarrassment was only just beginning for Haley. For there, standing on the Millers' doorstep, holding a basket full of breakfast goodies, was . . . Haley's unbelievably hot neighbor, Reese Highland.

What's he doing here! Haley thought, mortified.

"Um, hi," she said, biting her lip and smoothing out a strand of her auburn hair. It just grazed her shoulders these days, thanks to an emergency haircut over fall break.

"Merry Christmas," said Reese, flashing Haley an irresistible grin.

"So, um, I bet you're wondering why I'm wearing a panda dress," Haley said self-consciously.

Reese smiled and opened his barn jacket to reveal . . . a red and green reindeer chunky-knit sweater. "Let me guess," he said. "Your grandmother's in town too?"

Haley nodded. *Wow, leave it to Reese to look great in a sweater with felt antlers,* she thought, sighing.

"Well, I'm impressed you're actually wearing it," he said. "I can't imagine Coco De Clerq or Whitney Klein ever putting on something one of their grandmothers made them."

He was referring, of course, to Hillsdale's reigning teen queens, the most popular girls in the sophomore class, and at times the bane of Haley's existence.

"Then again," he added, "I think Coco's only living grandmother, Starla, is currently on her fifth husband in Texas. I seriously doubt she even knows how to sew."

Haley shrugged. *Ugh! What is wrong with me!* she wondered. *Why am I suddenly so tongue-tied around Reese?*

"Well, for what it's worth, I think it's pretty cool you're wearing that panda bear dress," he continued. "I find it very . . . attractive when a girl is this close to her family."

Haley was flabbergasted. Here was Reese Highland—gorgeous, perfect, super-smart, star of the varsity soccer and basketball teams Reese Highland—flirting with her on her stoop and all she could think of to say was "Um, thanks."

Reese and Haley had shared many moments like this one since the Millers had moved from Northern California to Hillsdale, New Jersey, at summer's end. In fact, they had grown quite close. But one un-expected delivery, an unfortunate panda sweater-dress, with three sets of googly eyes, and Haley was just as awkward around him as if they had just met.

"I guess I should probably get going," Reese said, though he seemed to be waiting for Haley to make the next move. "My mom just wanted me to bring over this homemade coffee cake. It's a Highland fam-ily tradition," he added, handing Haley the basket of goodies. Reese gave her a quick peck on the cheek, and she smiled at him sheepishly. "Well, tell your folks Merry Christmas," he said before hopping off the porch and heading back next door. "Hope the Millers have a great one."

Haley watched as he disappeared into the Highlands' house next door. *Ugh, I'm such an idiot*, she thought, now kicking herself for missing the opportunity to invite Reese inside to share a mug of hot Christmas cocoa. *What if that was my only chance to see him before the end of break?*

"Haley, come quick!" her dad called from the living room. "Gam Polly knitted Mitchell a raccoon suit!"

Relieved to be distracted from her Reese Highland angst, Haley turned to go back inside. *Poor Mitchell,* she thought, realizing there were worse gifts in the world than a panda sweaterdress.

While she hadn't gotten what she *really* wanted this year, so far, Haley had to admit, it had been an okay day. What she didn't realize, though, was that Christmas wasn't over yet. Not by a long shot.

Later that morning, Mitchell, still wearing his hooded raccoon outfit, pulled the last gift from under the tree. "It is. For. Haley," he said, handing her the package.

Perry was barely able to contain his excitement as Haley untied the silver ribbon and slid off the wrapping paper. She carefully opened the lid of the box and found inside . . . a brand-new digital camcorder, just like her dad's.

This was, in fact, the present Haley had been waiting for, ever since her dad had let her film a few sequences in Yellowstone and Glacier the previous summer. This was precisely the gift she would've asked for had she still been young enough to sit on Santa's lap. This was, Haley knew, her destiny. And now her Christmas was complete.

"Thank you, Daddy! Thank you, thank you, thank you," she said, rushing over to her father and hugging him around the neck.

"I figured it was about time you had your own equipment," he said, beaming. "Here, let me show you how it works." They sat down on the floor together and began poring over the instruction manual. It wasn't long before Haley had the camera on and filming. Her first subject was her napping grandmother, who was snoring more loudly than one of the bears she was so fond of knitting.

"Haley. Will you. Make a movie. About me," Mitchell asked, tugging on her sleeve until the phone rang.

"I'll get it," Joan said, popping up. "I've got to check on the turkey anyway."

Haley's mom disappeared into the kitchen, only to reemerge moments later. This time, she was throwing her hair up into a bun and slipping on her shoes. "Sorry, guys, but I have to go to the office," she said, pulling on a sweater.

"On Christmas Day?" Perry asked, frowning.

"It's that big case we've been working on, the one that goes to trial in January." Joan grabbed her purse and coat. "They just delivered a truckload of files on our doorstep. Figures, doesn't it, that those big corporate bullies would wait for a national holiday to disclose their evidence? We've only been asking for it for six weeks."

"Tell them. You can't go," said Mitchell.

"I can't, sweetie."

"Sure you can," said Perry.

Joan hesitated, then said, "My old firm has offered to help, and they're flying in a small team to stay through pretrial. I have to pick them up at the airport so we can start sifting through the material." She was now stuffing paperwork into a canvas tote. "How we're ever going to pull this thing off with just five of us to their team of fifty lawyers, I don't know."

"Who's coming in from San Francisco?" Perry asked, standing up.

Joan looked over at her husband. "Maggie, Les and . . . Peter," she said.

Haley noticed a strange look passing between her parents. It was a look she hadn't seen in the past six months, and certainly not since the Millers had moved to Hillsdale.

Gam snorted in her chair and rolled over.

"I love that this is the first I'm hearing of all this," Perry said in a harsh whisper before glancing at Haley and Mitchell, and then at his mother. "This is great, Joan, just great. What a way to spend the holidays."

"We can talk about it later," Joan said firmly. "I only just found out myself."

"Right," Perry said, picking up the newspaper and his slippers and storming upstairs—without saying goodbye to his wife.

It was only then that Haley realized she'd filmed the whole exchange. She turned the camera off and set it down, reaching for Mitchell's hand.

"You two will be okay here with Daddy and Gam Polly, won't you?" Joan asked brightly, kissing Haley and Mitchell on their cheeks.

"This is not. What Santa. Would want," Mitchell said, clinging to her leg.

"I'll be back soon. Promise. And then we can celebrate all over again," Joan said in an overly cheery tone. Haley couldn't help but detect a little guilt in her mother's voice, beneath its sunny overtones.

"Why does. She always. Have to go," Mitchell said as Joan flew out the door.

"It's hard work saving the world, Mitch," Haley said as they plopped down at their grandmother's feet. Mitchell snuggled up next to Haley. Their dalmatian, Freckles, snuggled up next to Mitchell. And they all watched the embers in the fireplace burn down as they drifted off to sleep.

Haley awoke from her nap to the smell of something burning and Freckles's barking. Then a smoke alarm sounded in the kitchen. Haley jumped up, ran into the other room and threw open the oven doors to find the once beautiful Christmas turkey now black as asphalt and spewing clouds of smoke.

Without hesitating, she turned the oven off, grabbed a pair of hot pads and moved the turkey to the sink, where she doused it with cool water. Then she hopped up on a stool and waved a damp cloth in front of the smoke detector to get it to stop its screeching. Crisis averted, Haley turned around to find Mitchell and Gam Polly staring up at her in awe.

"Haley is. My hero," Mitchell said robotically.

"I must have dozed off," Gam said. "Where is everyone? And what in the world happened to the turkey?"

"Who's burning? Where's the fire?" Perry shouted, bursting into the room wearing his bathrobe. "I turned off the shower and heard the alarm."

"Haley stopped. Dinner. From burning down. The house," said Mitchell.

"You've got a very resourceful, quick-thinking girl here, Perry," Gam Polly said, patting Haley on the back. "From the looks of that stove, the whole house could have gone up in flames."

"Haley, what were you thinking?" Perry demanded emphatically. "Let me see your arms." He grabbed her hands and inspected them front and back for any signs of burns.

"I'm all right," Haley said. She realized, though, that her dad was probably right to scold her. It had been a brave but very foolish thing to do.

"I'm just glad you're okay," said Perry, squeezing a little too tight. "What was your mother thinking, leaving the oven on?"

"Now what. Will. We do. For Christmas dinner," Mitchell asked.

"Well, we can't cook anything here," Gam said. "Not in this kitchen."

"Nothing'll be open on Christmas Day," Perry added.

"We could. Eat. Cereal," said Mitchell. Cereal was his favorite food.

"There is one place that's open on Christmas," Haley suggested. "In fact, it's open three hundred sixty-five days a year. It says so on their menus."

"What's that, dear?" Gam asked.

"The Golden Dynasty."

"Kids, go get dressed," Perry said, trying to sound positive. "We're having ourselves a Chinese Christmas."

The Golden Dynasty was, surprisingly, packed when the Miller clan—sans Joan—entered the restaurant. Irene Chen was working the register—not unusual, since her family owned the place. The potbellied Shaun and his cute shutterbug friend, Devon, were hanging out at the hostess station, keeping Irene company. Meanwhile, Whitney Klein and her mother were sharing a corner booth along with an enormous order of moo shu pork.

The newly sober Sasha was seated on the other side of the restaurant with her boyfriend—rocker Johnny Lane, the lead singer of the Hedon—and her mom, who had recently returned to Hillsdale after living in her native Paris for several years.

"Haley Miller got a cravin' for some sweet-and-sour Shaun this Christmas," Shaun said, grabbing his massive gut and doing a little dance around her. "What's shakin', sugar strut?"

"Hey," Haley said, smiling as she took off her jacket at the pack of artsy outsiders she knew from school. She suddenly realized she was still wearing the panda dress, but at this point, she didn't exactly care.

"We-he-hell," said Shaun. "Devon, looks like it's bear season in Hillsdale."

"Hey," Irene said without looking up from the countertop she was going over with a damp rag. "Nice dress," she added. Haley couldn't tell if she was being sarcastic or not. With Irene, either was a possibility.

"So, you coming to Devo's house for the ball drop on New Year's?" Shaun asked, nudging the shy Devon toward Haley. "We're sculpting snapper out of tofu and chomping on snow cones."

"Um, I'll think about it," Haley said, not quite sure what to make of the invitation. Especially since it hadn't come directly from Devon.

Haley followed her father and grandmother into the dining room.

"Ohmigosh, who let the dogs out?" Whitney asked as Haley and Mitchell passed by her table. "What's with the barnyard suits?"

"Actually, Whitney, we're in costume," Haley replied, thinking quickly as she took Mitchell's hand in solidarity. "We were, um, singing to orphans all day. We performed this, like, musical revue about a veterinarian at the orphanage, and it turned out, there was this big Hollywood producer there, um, picking up his newly adopted kid. And he, uh, well, he said he thinks we've got talent. And he's considering us for his next film. So we just came here to celebrate."

"No. Way," said Whitney, clearly overcome by jealousy. "So I'll see you at Richie Huber's for New Year's, right? It's gonna be a rager."

"Maybe," Haley said as she turned and dragged Mitchell toward where her dad and Gam were now sitting. She didn't usually like to lie, but she wasn't about to let Whitney pick on Mitchell. Especially not on Christmas Day.

● ● ●

How quickly the perfect family scene can devolve into an unmitigated disaster. Haley may have gotten what she wanted for Christmas this year. But the Millers' house nearly caught on fire. They're eating Chinese food instead of turkey on Christmas Day. Joan is off to work again, saving the environment instead of spending time with her family. And speaking of natural selection, Haley and Mitchell look as if they're on loan from the zoo.

Will Joan's passion for green living drive a wedge between her and her husband and kids in the coming months? Or will the Millers be able to hold on to their perfect, albeit quirky, nuclear family?

And what about Haley? What will the new year hold for her? Will her relationship with Reese continue to blossom? Or will she choose to make beautiful pictures with Devon instead? Or is there someone else altogether Haley is holding out for?

To send Haley to Devon's with Irene and Shaun for New Year's, turn to page 28. To have her go to Richie Huber's, where everyone else from school is likely to be, turn to page 17.

With both of Haley's parents preoccupied this season, she's about to find out how easy it is to bend the rules. But will she break them? Or establish new boundaries on her own? That, of course, is entirely up to you.

NEW YEAR'S EVE
AT RICHIE HUBER'S

**Someone always ends
up booting on
New Year's Eve.**

Haley decided to head to Richie Huber's on New Year's Eve to check out his "rager." It was, after all, right around the corner, which meant she could walk. And the other options for the evening—sitting at home and setting off sparklers on the porch with Gam Polly and Mitchell or begging for a ride across town to Devon's house in the Floods—weren't exactly appealing.

Still, walking those few blocks to Richie's was easier said than done. Especially since December in the Northeast had redefined the word *freezing* for

Haley. Before she had even reached the end of her driveway, a numbness was creeping into her fingers, toes and cheeks. By the time she made it to Richie's front door, she was certain frostbite was setting in.

Even so, as she rang the doorbell, Haley stripped off her big woolly hat, puffy coat and scarf. She didn't, after all, want to make an entrance looking like a wintry marshmallow. Even if her lips were about to turn blue.

She shoved her cold-weather armor into her bag, next to her new video camera. She didn't intend to film anything, but she brought it with her anyway because she shuddered to think what her little brother might do if left alone with it.

"Well, hello," a meathead senior in a baseball cap and a letterman jacket said to Haley as he opened the door. Haley stepped inside, over the mountain of winter coats piling up in the foyer.

"Hi," she shouted over the pumping bass.

In the adjoining living room and dining room, girls were dancing on tables in glittery party hats. Out back in the family room, a pack of varsity football guys chanted, "Drink! Drink! Drink!" while a skinny freshman boy chugged beer from a flower vase.

Haley began to wonder what she was doing here as she made her way through the packed house.

"Yo, bro," Freddy Chopper said to his buddy Garrett "the Troll" Noll as Haley attempted to squeeze by them. "I just quit wearing deodorant because I hear chicks dig your natural scent."

Oh, please, Haley thought. *There's nothing natural about your scent.*

"Dude, my pheromones are so primitive," the Troll countered, while taking a whiff of his own pits, "lady bears track me down in the woods."

"Excuse me," Haley said loudly, passing between them with her nose at armpit height. A horrible stench of body odor clung to the boys. *Those aren't pheromones,* Haley thought. *They're chemical weapons.*

At last she reached the back room, where she was surprised to spot Annie Armstrong, Dave Metzger and Hannah Moss sitting on the floor by the couch. *What are they doing at a Richie Huber party?* Haley wondered. And that was when she noticed that Annie and Dave were untangling a rat's nest of cables, while Hannah was testing mikes and three electronic keyboards.

Rubber Dynamite must be playing tonight, Haley realized. Dave and Hannah had a regular gig as the band's sound engineers, and Annie usually helped out to make sure the pair didn't get too . . . close.

"Hey, Haley!" Annie called out, clearly thrilled to see a friendly face.

"Hi," Haley said as Annie bounded over.

"I was going to call you earlier."

"Really?"

"Yeah, I need the last week of notes from English class."

"Annie, you were in school that week."

"It doesn't hurt to compare," Annie said defensively.

Ever since Haley had gotten an A on her last English paper (compared to Annie's A-), Annie had been paranoid about Haley eclipsing her in the class rankings.

"I'll think about it," Haley said, continuing to make her way through the crowd.

"Check out those imports," Spencer Eton said lustily from the kitchen as he gawked at some recent female arrivals. Judging by the girls' plaid miniskirts and white button-downs knotted at their waists, they were from St. Agnes, a nearby Catholic high school.

The St. Agnes girls, Haley had observed, seemed to always wear their uniforms, even when classes weren't in session and particularly when there was a Hillsdale High party to attend. Their pleated skirts and kneesocks never failed to attract the attention of Hillsdale's randy public school boys. With little effort, the St. Agnes girls inevitably ended up getting their pick of senior hotties.

"I'll give you something to repent!" Richie called out to them.

The girls rolled their eyes and left in search of less offensive company, opening up a clear line of sight through the crowd for Haley.

Cool shot, she thought, reaching into her bag for the video camera. She hadn't really been planning to document the party, but given that Reese was nowhere to be found, and given that she currently had nothing better to do, why not?

Love is in the air, Haley noted, spotting two

couples through her lens. Drew Napolitano and Cecily Watson were standing close together, totally in sync, with their arms and fingers intertwined. *Guess Whitney lost out in her bid to win back Drew's affections,* Haley thought as she watched him whisper something in Cecily's ear. *She should've locked that up when she had the chance.* Sasha Lewis and Johnny Lane, meanwhile, were leaning against a wall with their hands in each other's back pockets. *So . . . freakin' . . . cool,* Haley thought, admiring the pair. *Though I'm surprised she got him to come if Rubber Dynamite is playing.*

Haley panned across the room to a giant pyramid of empty beer cans that was teetering atop the kitchen table. The drunken host and his legions of hangers-on were now standing around it, marveling at the architectural feat as Matthew Graham steadied his hand and prepared to place the next can on the top tier.

"Wait a second!" Coco slurred, staggering into the frame.

Coco's drinking? Haley was shocked to realize. She zoomed in on the shot glass in one of Coco's hands, then on the empty champagne glass in the other. *What's she doing?* Haley wondered. While Coco De Clerq rarely missed a Richie Huber party, she almost never drank at them. *Ah, but it's New Year's,* Haley remembered, recalling Spencer's and Whitney's multiple cracks that Coco indulged but once a year.

"Before Graham cracker knocks over this beautiful

sliver monumess," Coco said fuzzily, "I'd like to dedi-
cate it to . . ." Just then, she glanced up and saw
Haley's video camera trained right on her. "Haley
Miller?"

Coco lunged forward, bumping a corner of the
pyramid. The whole castle of cans came crashing
down around her.

"You did not just do that!" Richie cried out in
disbelief, followed by the irritated moans of a few
onlookers. He chucked one of the cans against the
wall. "That was about to be a Huber house record."

"Nice party foul, Co-Ho," Spencer said, anointing
Coco with a new nickname.

"Ah, shove it up your tailpipe, Richie," Coco said,
staggering toward Haley. "And you too, Spencer Eton."

Haley bashfully lowered the camcorder and tried
to recede into the background, but it was no use.

"I wanna talk to you, Miller," Coco slurred. "You
can keep filming. It's okay if you're obthessthed with
me, Haley. Everyone is."

Haley shrugged and turned the camera back on,
focusing in on Coco.

"Get a clue, De Clerq!" a senior named Jed
Harvey shouted from across the room.

"That's right, Jed. You know you wannit," Coco
yelled back, cocking her hip and giving the camera a
haughty look.

Wow, Haley thought. *She's really a sloppy drunk*.

"Don't you get it, Co-Ho?" Jed shouted. "You're
last semester's news. Everyone knows you're locked

together at the knees. Unlike your sister. Now, there's a girl who knows how to have fun."

At that point, one of his friends chimed in, "Ali Cat! Rrrrr!" He was referring, of course, to Coco's older and much faster sister, Alison De Clerq.

"I can have fun," Coco said, picking up a vodka bottle from the kitchen table and taking a big swig.

"Ooh, ooh, ooh, I love being on camera!" Whitney exclaimed, bouncing over to refill Coco's flute with more champagne and smiling for Haley. "I'm very photogenic."

"Ah, more beverages," Coco said, taking a sip of champagne and hiccuping loudly.

"Only I always forget which is my best side," Whitney added, concentrating hard and tilting her head in one direction, then another. "Ooh, I've got an idea!" she said, turning to face Coco. "Let's have Haley make a show about us! Like real-life TV!"

"It's called re-al-i-ty," Coco said witheringly, before hiccuping again. "Something you, Whitney, would know nothing about. Isn't she so out of touch?" Coco directed her question at the camera, then reached for the vodka bottle once again.

"Had enough yet?" Spencer asked.

"I've only just begun," Coco said, sneering at him.

"I knew one of these New Year's Eves you'd take it too far," he said, pulling up a chair to watch as the wound-tight Coco completely unraveled. "Ladies and gentlemen, zero hour has arrived."

"Are you still filming?" Coco asked Haley, who nodded from behind the camera. A crowd was beginning to form. At that moment, Coco grabbed . . . Reese Highland.

Ohmigosh! Haley thought. *Where did he come from?*

"C'mere, Highland," Coco slurred. "I want to interview you for my very own talk show." She nudged him toward a couch, and Reese looked at Haley as if to ask, *What the heck is going on?*

"Reese, you and I are the two most pop-a-lar people in the sophomore class," Coco said.

"Not after tonight!" a senior called out.

"Coco, maybe you should take it easy, huh?" Reese said.

"Nonsense," Coco continued, pretending to hold up a microphone. "You and me, we're the most pop-a-lar people in the sophomore class. So. Why aren't we dating?"

Haley's jaw dropped. She didn't know whether to keep filming Coco's embarrassing antics, or stop the camera and slap some sense into her.

Then again, like every other girl in the room, Haley wanted to know just what Reese would say.

"I don't think this is really the time or place for this kind of talk," Reese said, trying to put Coco off.

"C'mon, Highland. Inquiring minds wanna know," Coco said, holding the pretend microphone in his face. The crowd hushed as they all waited for Reese's response. "Why would you turn down the hottest girl in school?" Coco pressed. "Or do you just not like girls? Is that it? Because you know that's what some people say."

At that moment, Haley wanted to strangle Coco De Clerq.

"Well, Coco," Reese began tentatively. "If you insist on having this conversation here and now . . . I think you're a really great girl and all. You're just not the girl for me. There's someone else I've got my eye on." He turned to look straight at the camera, through the lens and into Haley's eyes.

Haley nearly dropped her camcorder. The only thing that kept it glued to her face was the fear of having half the school see just how red her cheeks currently were.

"Fine. I don't need you anyway," Coco said, grabbing hold of Haley's arm and dragging her and the camera out of the room. Whitney scrambled to follow them. "Where's Spencer?" Coco demanded.

"I think I saw him go upstairs," one of the St. Agnes girls replied. "With your sister."

"That little . . . ," Coco muttered. She pulled Haley up the stairs with her, then threw open the first bedroom door she came to.

"Who's the ho now, huh?" Coco bellowed as she flipped on the overhead lights. April Doyle and Jed Harvey were rolling around on top of the covers.

"Oops, sorry," Whitney said as she closed the door. "Wrong make-out session."

Coco threw open the next door, which turned out

to be a linen closet. "Well, I wonder who could be behind door number three," she said, bursting into the third room off the hall and shouting, "You dirty little slut! You're a disgrace to the De Clerq family name."

Whitney hit the light switch. In Richie Huber's bedroom, Ali and Spencer were slouching on a sofa, fully clothed. There was a bong sitting between them, and a cloud of gray smoke hovered in the air above their heads.

"Ew, what's that funny smell?" Whitney asked, cocking her head.

"Ugh," Coco moaned, her face turning green. Before anyone could stop her, and with the camera still rolling, Coco vomited all over Richie Huber's bed.

● ● ●

Quelle horreur!

Guess Coco's decision to have a little champagne fun on New Year's didn't go quite as well as planned. She managed to publicly humiliate herself, prove definitively that Reese Highland is just not that into her, and then to top it all off, she just puked in the host's bed. Not exactly a happy new year.

Coco is used to being the control freak, not the freak show. If you think Haley feels bad for the dethroned homecoming princess, have her stick around and lend a helping hand in the bathroom, where Coco will be praying to the porcelain gods, on page 43.

When the clock strikes midnight, kisses will fly, but will they for Haley and Reese Highland? If you think Haley shouldn't miss the countdown to New Year's just because Coco's night was ruined, have Haley return to the party, where Reese, Sasha and Cecily are waiting, on page 36.

If you think that video footage of Coco knocking over the pyramid of beer cans, trying to coerce Reese Highland into a love confession and puking in Richie's bed must be shared, have Haley go home, post Coco's drunken rampage on the Internet and promote the demise of "Co-Ho" on page 49.

Lastly, if you believe in the adage "what goes around comes around" and don't want to risk any bad karma for Haley, play it safe and head to English class on page 54.

Now that Coco De Clerq has been unseated as the sophomore class's reigning teen queen, will Haley step in and assume her role? What if . . . Haley Miller got the guy, the right friends and the admiration of the whole school? Would she even know what to do with all that power?

Charity begins at home—in this case, at the home of Devon McKnight.

Haley's dad pulled up to the McKnights' tiny clapboard house in the heart of the Floods, which was not at all what Haley was expecting. She knew that Devon's family wasn't as well-off as Shaun's or Irene's or even her own, but this was practically destitution.

The McKnights' house could have fit inside the Millers' two-car garage, and the "yard" was really just a narrow patch of brown grass running along the edge of the street. Run-down matchbox houses on either side of Devon's were practically touching his, and the neighbors to the left had a chain-link and barbed-wire fence and a mean-looking dog that growled in Perry and Haley's direction.

"You having second thoughts about this?" Haley's dad asked reassuringly. "You know you can always come back home and celebrate New Year's with Gam, Mitch and me. We're having a sparkling juice toast at midnight."

"No, it's okay, Dad. Really," Haley said, climbing out of the Millers' hybrid SUV. "I'll call you if I want to come home before twelve-thirty. And thanks for letting me stay out so late."

"You got it," he said. "I just want you to have a good time, Haley. I know things have been difficult at home lately, what with your mom working so much. But it'll settle down once she's won her case." He seemed to be trying to convince himself of this more than Haley.

Haley walked up to the front door and knocked as her dad started the engine. Irene greeted her at the door. She was dressed slightly more festively than usual, in a black baby-doll dress with black tights and combat boots.

Haley looked down at her own holey jeans, white tank top and green sequined cardigan. *For once, I'm the one who's underdressed,* she thought. *I wonder who Irene's trying to impress?*

Before stepping inside, Haley turned and waved to her dad, then watched as he pulled away, driving back toward the other side of town and the Millers' comfy house near the Heights.

"Come on. We better get into the kitchen and help the boys," Irene said, dragging Haley into the other room. "Shaun's creating an underwater paradise out of vegetables and bean curd, and he's planning to devour his tofu 'Atlantis' by midnight."

"So I take it he's still on his professional eating kick?" Haley asked.

"Yep," said Irene. Shaun had recently decided he could make a living stuffing hot dogs down his craw on the international professional eating circuit. He claimed the money he would win would subsidize his art.

"Well, I guess if his new career path doesn't work out, he can always take up sumo wrestling," Haley offered.

"If he puts on any more weight, he might as well move to Japan," Irene said emphatically. "Because I won't be speaking to him."

"Well, at least you were able to convince him to go vegetarian for his training," Haley added, trying to sound positive. "He might even lose weight scarfing down vegetables and tofu."

The McKnights' "kitchen" was actually more like a large closet with a stove. An old sheet served as the door, and there was open shelving to hold plates, cups and canned goods.

A frail-looking blond girl who must have been about Mitchell's age was perched on the only bit of countertop, wearing a sweater and dress that looked vaguely familiar to Haley. "Haley, this is Shana, Devon's sister," Irene explained.

"Hi, Shana," Haley said, shaking the little girl's delicate hand. Shana smiled and blinked her pale blue eyes.

"My parents work a lot of nights and holidays," Devon added. "So Shana and I get to spend a lot of time together. Don't we, kid?" Shana nodded.

It was at that moment that Haley recognized the sweater and dress. They were part of a package the Millers had sent to a "needy child" with the initials S. M., after picking her name off the "giving tree" at the mall. Suddenly, Haley felt ashamed of having been the slightest bit embarrassed by the panda bear dress she'd gotten for Christmas.

"Hey, hoss," Shaun said, scooping up Shana. "What do you say we go start calling for the new year? It won't come unless we ask for it." Irene and Haley followed them into the den/Devon's bedroom, where another old sheet separated a twin bed and dresser from a sofa-and-TV setup that served as the only communal family space in the house, apart from the tiny kitchen.

Despite the room's size, it was an appealing space. Artful snapshots, framed in cheap art-store clip frames, covered the walls, and there was a large sketched family portrait pinned to a bulletin board above the sofa. Haley recognized the photography and drawing as Devon's work.

"Hey, have you guys thought about what you're going to do for your midterm project in Mr. Von's class?" Haley asked. Shaun and Irene looked at each other, smiled, then looked at Haley and shook their heads. They both seemed to have a pretty good idea of what they'd be working on, though neither one of them was talking. "Fine, be that way," Haley said in a mocking tone. "I won't tell you what I'm working on either."

Actually, Haley had no idea what her project was going to be. Not yet anyway.

"Shouldn't you be worrying about that big English paper you have due in honors?" Irene countered. "I warned you about taking those brownnoser classes."

"Haley can't help it if she gots the heavy gray matter," said Shaun.

"I think she's just happy to be in a class with Reese Highland," Irene teased. Haley blushed. She was glad Devon wasn't in the room to hear this.

"D'oh!" Shaun added. "Looks like the Devo's got a stock car sneaking up on his bumper."

"Very funny," Haley said, casting a disapproving glance at Shaun and Irene. "Reese's car isn't even in the race."

That, of course, was a lie. The truth was, Haley wasn't sure who she liked better, Devon or Reese. And it was becoming increasingly difficult to decide.

Haley's cell phone vibrated. It was Annie Armstrong texting her. "U won't believe what just happened at Richie Huber's way cool NYE party! Coco De Clerq is . . . wasted. She just confessed her undying love for . . . Reese Highland. And! . . . he blew her off! Now she's . . . ohmigosh! Coco just threw up on Richie's bed! Gotta run, this is priceless! I've got to go find a video camera."

Interesting, Haley thought. *What the heck is Annie doing at Richie Huber's for New Year's? And if Reese doesn't like Coco, that must mean . . .*

"Shaun, you ready for your meatless feast?" Devon asked, bringing in the large tray of healthy snacks constructed to look like an undersea tableau. There were celery stick and nonfat cream cheese "mermaids"; "cockleshells" made out of carrots and peppers; artichoke heart "coral," and three giant "red snappers" constructed out of tofu, with radish "scales."

"Stand back, y'all. This is gonna get messy," Shaun said, holding his hands behind his back so that Devon could tie them with string. He leaned forward into starting position, and Devon picked up the stopwatch, stared at the face for a moment and shouted, "Go!"

Shaun tore into the snappers first, mowing through them until he had sucked those areas of the tray clean. Then he tackled the mermaids and seashells, which took a little more time to chew. Finally, he finished off the artichoke hearts, rooting around them like a pig sniffing out truffles.

Shana erupted in a spasm of laughter as she watched. "And time!" Devon shouted, holding up the stopwatch once Shaun had finished off the last of the veggies. "Two minutes, fifteen seconds. Not bad. Not bad at all."

"Shoot. Them stalk sirens slowed me down," Shaun said, motioning to the remnants of a celery mermaid.

"Now what are we going to eat?" Shana asked, throwing her hands up in the air.

"Don't worry, squirt," said Devon. "I saved some grub for us."

As they all piled onto the sofa to watch the Times Square countdown and snack on veggie sticks and dip, Haley couldn't help but be distracted by what Irene had said earlier.

As Haley watched Devon tickle his giggling sister, a big part of her wanted to be with him. He was sweet. He cared about his family. And whenever he kissed Haley, she felt real heat.

But what if . . . she was meant to be with Reese? Which boy did she belong with? The wholesome guy next door? Or the artistic, talented and somewhat complicated guy from the other side of the tracks?

That looming question was enough to make Haley wish that someone else would just choose her destiny for her. . . .

● ● ●

Well, that was certainly a telling trip to the Floods. Devon's family life is oh-so-different from Haley's. His parents work around the clock. He's constantly taking care of a shy younger sibling.

Then again, maybe Haley's and Devon's lives aren't so different after all.

But are these two meant to be more than just friends? Will their love of photography and filmmaking lead to a serious bond? Or will Haley find she's always thinking of something—or someone—else?

And with deadlines looming for her honors English paper and her art project, which one should she focus on first?

The clock is ticking, which means it's time to make some decisions. To have Haley rush over to Richie Huber's to find Reese before midnight, turn to page 36. To have Haley play it cool and wait to see Reese in English class in a few days, turn to page 54. Keep Haley close to Devon, Shaun and Irene by having her work on her art project on page 63. Or send Haley to Richie Huber's to help film Coco's downfall and post it on the Internet on page 49.

The best thing about a new year? It's a great time to start all over again.

MIDNIGHT MADNESS

The only way New Year's Eve is anticlimactic is if you have unrealistic expectations.

Whitney held Coco's hair back with one hand and pinched her own nose with the other as Coco dry-heaved into Richie's whirlpool tub. Finally, another round of vomit sputtered out of the formerly popular princess.

"That's it," Whitney said, patting her on the back. "Don't breathe through your nose. It'll burn," she advised.

"Of course you would know that, Whitney," Coco said, wiping her nose with the tissue Whitney offered her. "You are, after all, an expert in vomiting."

She turned to address Haley. "You, get me some ginger ale."

Haley considered Coco's demand. *Why would I spend my first New Year's Eve in Hillsdale serving her ruined highness soft drinks and saltine crackers,* she wondered. *Whitney's her best friend, and she seems to have everything under control.* "Actually, Coco, I think I'll head back to the party. Maybe if you'd said please." Haley turned on her heel and sauntered out of the room as Coco began to dry-heave again.

Back downstairs, everyone was packed into the back room, huddled around a makeshift stage that was set up with keyboards and amps. *Rubber Dynamite must be coming on any minute,* Haley realized.

Scanning the crowd, Haley looked for her friends, but she couldn't even spot Annie and Dave. *Maybe I should just walk home and watch the ball drop with Mitchell,* she thought with a sinking feeling.

Haley grabbed her bag and took out her coat. She plowed through the kitchen, where Spencer, Richie, Toby and Matt Graham were drinking beers and playing cards.

"Where are you off to?" Matt asked, reaching out to grab Haley's arm. "Don't you know midnight's almost here?" Matt often flirted with Haley, but she never knew whether or not to take him seriously.

"Yeah, I thought we were going to ring it in together, Miller," Richie added, grabbing her other arm.

Ugh, no way, Haley thought, looking at Richie's yellow, tobacco-stained teeth. *You're like a toad who never turns into a prince, no matter how many kisses you get.*

Suddenly, Haley spotted Reese Highland smiling at her from the back door. "Happy New Year, fellows," she blurted out to the boys in the kitchen, grabbing a noisemaker from the table and blowing it hard so that Richie and Matt would let go.

"I was wondering where you disappeared to," Reese said as Haley approached.

"I was trying to get away from all the wastoids," said Haley, taking a deep breath of fresh, non-vomit-infused air.

"I know," said Reese. "It's not exactly the way I'd pictured spending my New Year's Eve." Haley nodded. "So, you want to get out of here?" he asked. Haley nodded again, and smiled.

Sasha, Johnny, Drew and Cecily were waiting for them in the driveway. "Finally," Johnny said impatiently. "I thought you were going to subject me to Rubber Dynamite. You know that stuff makes my ears bleed." Johnny, who headed up the Hedon, had no interest in listening to a rival band's performance.

"Want to head back to my place for the countdown?" Reese asked.

"Sure," Sasha said brightly. "Good to see you, Haley," she added, smiling at her friend.

"Can we get going already?" Cecily asked, snuggling up against Drew's chest. "It's freezing out here! My native Hawaiian blood can't take it."

"Gladly," said Haley, linking arms with Reese. "Hello, you're talking to a Cali girl."

They walked back to Reese's, passing by the Miller residence, which was completely dark. Not a single light was on in the house. *Guess no one is waiting up for me,* she realized. *Looks like I won't be rushing home for curfew.*

"Where are your parents tonight?" Cecily asked Reese as he unlocked the front door and let everyone inside.

"They're out with my mom," Sasha responded for him.

"The Sorbonne connection lives on," Reese added.

"It's some charity event," said Sasha. "Haley, they asked your parents to come, but your mom said she was busy?"

"She has a big case coming up," Haley explained.

"And she's working on New Year's Eve?" Drew added. "That's intense. You know they say whatever you're doing at midnight on New Year's dictates how you'll spend the rest of the year."

"I sure hope not," Haley muttered, reluctant to spend an entire year with her mom working impossible hours and her parents hardly seeing each other.

The group gravitated to the Highlands' den and settled down on the leather club chairs. Haley warmed her toes underneath a plaid wool blanket while Reese started a fire in the fireplace, and the other girls cuddled up with their boyfriends for warmth.

"Make yourselves at home," Reese said, disappearing briefly into the kitchen. He returned with a plate of homemade holiday cookies. "You guys want some? I can't eat another one of these things or I will spontaneously combust."

Haley bit into a crescent-shaped cookie with powdered sugar on top, which was crisp on the outside and a little chewy on the inside. "Okay, maybe I'll have one," Reese said, grabbing a chocolate chip cookie and taking a bite.

"Reese?" Sasha asked in an overly sweet tone that implied she was about to ask a favor. "Do you still have that old guitar we used to bang around on when we were kids? I don't remember seeing it when I stayed here."

"You want it?" Reese asked. "I'll gladly hand it over. That case takes up half my closet."

"I might be willing to take it off your hands," Sasha said, glancing at Johnny. "This one's been teaching me a few chords."

Haley couldn't be sure, but she thought she recognized the expression on Johnny's face. For maybe the first time since she had known him, he looked really happy.

Johnny looked up at the old grandfather clock in the Highlands' den, then took Sasha's hand and led her into the dining room. Drew whispered something in Cecily's ear, and she giggled flirtatiously. "Um, we'll see you guys in a bit," Cecily said as they headed off to the kitchen.

"Well, guess that means it's almost midnight," Haley said, pretending not to hear Cecily's and Drew's lips smacking in the next room. She was already all too aware that she and Reese were the only people in the house not feverishly making out at the moment.

"So, you're coming to our first home basketball game next week, right?" Reese asked her. "Man, I can't wait for the season to get started. We've got such an awesome team this year. Drew really progressed over the summer, and Johnny keeps nailing those threes. It's going to be great."

He must know that I want to kiss him, Haley thought as she kept looking for any sign that Reese felt the same way. "Isn't Mrs. Eton's campaign fundraiser that night?" Haley asked, teasing Reese with the possibility she might not be in the bleachers cheering him on.

"Oh, come on," he said. "You can't miss the first game of the season. What sort of Hawk spirit is that? Besides, we can't even vote yet. And call me crazy, but something tells me you won't be donating a few grand to Mrs. Eton's gubernatorial campaign."

"Good point," Haley agreed. She heard the minute hand of the grandfather clock inch closer to the twelve.

Reese got up and stoked the fire, then came to sit on the arm of Haley's chair.

"Hi," she whispered, looking up at him adoringly.

"Hi," he said. And as the clock struck twelve,

Reese Highland leaned down and kissed Haley Miller, right on the lips.

● ● ●

Well, how's that for a start to a happy new year?

If you think Haley should continue to give Reese the full-court press, go to the first home basketball game and show support on page 74.

If you're more concerned with Haley's family life at the moment, since it's unlike Joan and Perry not to wait up for their daughter on New Year's Eve, have Haley head home on page 69.

Finally, if you want Haley to take advantage of a rare opportunity to mix with high-society Hillsdale, have her make an appearance at the Etons' campaign fund-raiser on page 82.

Life moves fast in Hillsdale. You have to act quickly if you don't want it to pass you by.

TAKE CARE OF COCO

A person's true colors
aren't always pretty.

"Gross," Whitney said squeamishly, wrinkling her nose in disgust as Coco dashed into Richie's bathroom and threw up again. And again. And again.

Soon she was only dry-heaving.

Haley followed Coco into the bathroom and held back her hair for her as she puked into the empty whirlpool tub.

"Ugh, I can't deal with this right now," Ali De Clerq announced, storming out of the room.

"You're her sister," Whitney called after Ali. "You can't leave her like this."

"Whatever, Whitney," Ali said from the hall. "It's not like you haven't had any experience with 'the repeats.' Anyway, it looks like the new girl has volunteered to do all the dirty work."

"Later, Co-Ho," Spencer said, getting up to follow Ali out the door. He paused and added, "You know, Coco, if you weren't such a lush tonight, maybe you would have finally figured out that Ali and I are just friends."

"Ha!" Whitney exclaimed. "I've seen you two hook up."

"When?" Spencer demanded. "All you've seen is two people trying to help each other get over their mutual misery caused by none other than Coco De Clerq. Well, guess what. I'm definitely over it now." And with that, Spencer walked out of the room.

"Why don't we try to hit the toilet next time," Haley gently coached Coco as she steered her over to the commode. She figured throwing up down the tub drain probably wasn't the best or most sanitary idea.

"My mouth is not going anywhere near that toilet seat," Coco slurred as she returned to her post, hovering over the tub. She spit up again and whimpered pathetically, "Look at me, I'm hideous."

Haley put her hand on Coco's sweaty back and said, "There, there. It's not so bad. You'll feel better . . . in a couple of days."

Whitney, meanwhile, had left the bathroom and taken a seat at Richie's desk, where she was flipping through a men's magazine swimsuit issue. "Check out this 'kini,'" Whitney called out. "Coco, we should really talk about where we're going for spring break this year. I mean, when you're done hurling your brains out."

"Haley, make me a promise," Coco said remorsefully as the alcohol left her body and she finally started to sober up. "Swear on your life you'll never show that video to anyone."

"Of course," Haley assured her.

"Ugh, I made such a fool of myself tonight," Coco went on. "I'll be the first person in Hillsdale history to go from most popular girl in the sophomore class to laughingstock, literally overnight."

"It's unfortunate," Haley said, "but everyone seems to go through an embarrassing moment like this one way or another."

"And I picked the hard way."

"That's why they call it hard alcohol," Whitney interjected. "Because it's a hard lesson to learn."

"People have really short memories," Haley said to Coco. "I'm sure they'll forget all about it."

"In a couple of months." Coco sighed.

At that moment, Ali barged into the room, carrying a tall glass of water and saltine crackers. "Here, I thought you could use these," she said, handing the refreshments to Coco and turning to leave.

"Wait," Coco said, setting down the glass of water and grabbing her sister's arm. "Thanks."

"Whatever," Ali said, shrugging her off.

"I'm really . . . sorry, Ali," Coco added. "I've been pretty awful to you, haven't I?"

Haley was shocked. It was the first time on record that Coco De Clerq was apologizing, and what's more, it seemed as if she actually meant it.

"So is it true that you and Spencer never hooked up?" Whitney, in her usual blunt style, asked.

"Come on, do you really think I'd fool around with a sophomore?" Ali asked.

Coco added, "So all those rumors . . ."

"Were just that, rumors," said Ali. "At a certain point, you just quit fighting the tide, and let people believe whatever they want to believe about you." She turned to look at Coco. "I just never thought you'd be one of them."

"But you two were always sneaking off together," Coco said.

"Yeah, to talk about you," Ali explained. "Did you know he's been crazy in love with you for the past two and a half years? Probably not, because you're always chasing after Reese Highland. Wake up, Coco. Your beloved Reese has got it bad for your little redheaded friend over there." Haley blushed, but the comment was lost on Coco, who was deep in thought.

"Spencer Eton," Coco said absently. "In love with me." Haley could tell Coco's mind was racing back to all those moments when Spencer must have tried to tell her how he felt, only to get scared and give in to his sarcastic streak instead.

46

"Well, not anymore," Ali replied. "He gave up on you about a month ago. Went cold turkey. Now he couldn't care less if you were living or dead."

"Ugh, I've been such an idiot," said Coco, resting her head down on the side of the tub. "All this time . . . It wasn't Reese I wanted. It was Spencer."

"Maybe it's not too late," Haley offered.

"We could crash the Etons' fund-raiser next week," Whitney suggested. "I hear they're expecting famous people. Wouldn't that be fun?"

"Isn't that the same night as the first home basketball game?" Haley asked gingerly. But no one seemed to hear her.

"It might work," Coco said, holding on to the slightest glimmer of hope. "Maybe he still does have feelings for me."

Haley hated to say it, but given the look on Spencer's face when he had stormed out of Richie's room earlier, there was little chance of that.

● ● ●

When the mighty fall, they fall fast and hard.

That was certainly a generous act on Haley's part. Coco De Clerq hasn't exactly been nice to Haley Miller since she arrived in Hillsdale. But when Coco was down and out, Haley was there to help.

If you think Haley should continue hanging out with the party girls and find out if Coco's really changed her stripes, turn to page 82.

If you feel like watching Reese, Johnny, Sebastian

and Drew Napolitano drive to the hoop at the first home basketball game, flip to page 74.

Lastly, if you think enough is enough with the social obligations, have Haley head home on page 69.

Political correctness, athletic prowess or Miller family togetherness: Take your pick. Just don't be surprised if your decision draws out a different side of Haley.

SECRETS ON VIDEO

It's easy to get caught in the World Wide Web.

Haley came back from Richie Huber's party to a pitch-black house. She was ten minutes early for curfew, not that anyone was around to take note. *Thanks for waiting up,* she thought, letting herself in and flipping on the porch lights.

I should have stayed at the party, she thought, noticing that her mother's car wasn't in the garage and that her dad was upstairs snoring in her parents' room.

Haley closed her bedroom door behind her, took her camcorder out of her bag and placed it on the desk next to her computer. She connected a cable from the video input to the USB port on her laptop and waited.

Showtime, Haley thought as the computer chimed, signaling that the download had been successfully completed. She put in earphones and pressed Play.

Scene by scene, Haley watched the debauchery unfold. She couldn't believe the footage she'd captured of Coco De Clerq's downfall. As she watched the clip where Coco toppled over the pyramid of beer cans and the moment Spencer coined the nickname "Co-Ho," she had to cover her mouth to keep from laughing hysterically and waking up the whole house. *Coco is going to die when she sees this,* she thought gleefully. *And so will the rest of the school.*

Haley couldn't stop herself from hitting Rewind every time Reese Highland appeared on-screen. Especially during the part where he reluctantly rejected Coco right to her face. Seeing it for the third time still didn't feel like enough.

Just when Haley thought the performance couldn't get any better, Coco began her jealous rant and barged in on Spencer and Ali, who were getting high, not getting it on. Then came the icing on the cake: Coco projectile-vomiting all over Richie Huber's bed, and then into his huge whirlpool tub.

It was more than all of Coco De Clerq's many enemies combined could've hoped for.

Infamous, Haley concluded as the docudrama came to a close.

There are just a few things I should do before I up-load, she thought. *What if . . . I copied Coco's vomit scene and pasted it back in five times in a row, like so?*

Haley created a loop, so Coco threw up over and over again as if in an instant replay. *I bet it would look even more disgusting in slow mo,* she decided as she decreased the speed of the playback.

There! Haley thought, finally satisfied. With a single click, Haley fired the video off into cyberspace.

Before she fell asleep that night, she sighed with contentment, feeling she'd avenged the innocent and defenseless people of Hillsdale High. She fancied herself a Robin Hood who filmed the rich to amuse the poor, and protected the Annie Armstrongs, Dave Metzgers, Irene Chens, Sasha Lewises and Johnny Lanes of the world.

Take that, Co-Ho, she thought, semiconsciously.

The next day, the moment Coco laid eyes on the video, she knew exactly who was responsible. Coco informed her father what Haley Miller had done. Maurice De Clerq didn't waste a second before contacting his heavy-hitting attorneys.

But no matter what the De Clerq legal team did to stop it, there seemed to be no way to squash the video. *Co-Ho Uncensored* was the most popular video downloaded in Hillsdale for months. Even after Haley took it off the Internet, figuring that Coco had learned her lesson, the file had already become viral and been saved to hard drives everywhere.

At first, Haley was proud of her short film. She couldn't deny that it felt nice getting five-star ratings from viewers online and having the kids at school treat her like a cult hero. Even Mr. Von, the art teacher, appreciated the atypical camera angles she used.

But then, a week after *Co-Ho*'s debut, Mrs. Eton received a threatening phone call from one of her opponents' campaign manager. Spencer had been identified as the guy smoking pot in the video. This, needless to say, wasn't exactly a help to Mrs. Etons' bid for governor.

In the ensuing weeks and months leading up to elections, ads on prime-time TV featured Haley's clip of Spencer sitting under a dark cloud of pot smoke. An angry voice-over intoned, "Eleanor Eton claims to have good family values. Meet her only child, Spencer. If this is how she raises her son, how will she mess up New Jersey's future?"

When Mrs. Eton lost the election, Haley knew she was indirectly responsible. She was left to harbor the guilt, not to mention the loneliness that descended after her classmates turned on her. Turns out, Spencer Eton had a lot more friends at Hillsdale than either Coco *or* Haley. Haley spent the rest of her years at Hillsdale High experiencing life as a has-been film producer—she was never quite able to replicate the success of *Co-Ho Uncensored*.

What's worse, Reese abandoned her after he found out she had posted her video of Coco online.

While he acknowledged that Coco had pulled some mean tricks in her day, he told Haley he thought she had stooped even lower, and that he was no longer proud to be seen with her.

So not only did Haley lose all her friends, her reputation and her self-respect, she lost the one guy who really mattered to her.

● ● ●

Hang your head and go back to page l.

HONORS ENGLISH

The only thing harder than getting to the head of the class? Staying at the head of the class.

Haley's honors English teacher, Ms. Lipsky, wasn't what you'd call an imposing woman. She wore her mousy brown hair either braided or pinned in a librarianesque bun on top of her head. Her horn-rimmed glasses hid most of her face. And her boxy denim jumpers and fuzzy gray sweaters disguised any curves in her womanly figure.

At times, Haley thought Ms. Lipsky seemed like the least imposing figure on campus. Except, of course, when it came to handing out grades.

Somewhere between marking up papers with red ink and publicly denouncing her students' faults and weaknesses, Ms. Lipsky found all the confidence she lacked in daily life. Students withered under her gaze as she ruined yet another of Hillsdale High's perfect 4.0 GPAs.

On this particular morning, she was preparing to pass back a set of term papers to her sophomore honors English class. Haley nervously bit the end of her pencil, wondering what to expect.

Ms. Lipsky grabbed the stack of term papers and paced around the room. "Ms. Armstrong," she said, stopping in front of Annie's desk and raising an eyebrow as she cocked her hip. "A very . . . thorough effort, as usual, dissecting the marriage of fellow Romantics Mary and Percy Bysshe Shelley. However," Ms. Lipsky added, delivering Annie's book-length term paper to her desk with a thud, "once again your thesis drowns in a sea of information." Annie looked at the B- on her title page and sank down in her chair.

"And as for you, David," Ms. Lipsky said, turning to face squirrelly Dave Metzger, who was sitting next to Annie, his girlfriend of several months, "I'm appalled you would let Ms. Armstrong edit your term paper. Everything about this project—your chosen topic, your sentence structure, the whole foundation of your argument—blatantly echoes her work. Bad form." Dave smiled feebly at Annie, then cringed when he saw his D.

Ms. Lipsky moved on to Sasha. "Ms. Lewis, I must say, I'm most impressed with your turnaround these last few weeks." Without further comment, she dropped a B+ paper onto Sasha's desk before proceeding on to Reese.

Haley felt pangs of sympathy as Ms. Lipsky slowly circled Reese's desk, knitting her eyebrows together in a curious expression. "This was a very clever perspective, Mr. Highland," she finally said, "examining themes of travel in Elizabethan poetry. Your economy of language was commendable." She handed Reese's slim paper back with a big B+ written at the top. "Perhaps you should consider loaning this to Ms. Armstrong and Mr. Metzger as a reference before they jointly begin their next assignment?"

Annie quietly fumed at her desk.

Ms. Lipsky next paused in front of skinny Dale Smithwick. Dale, the dark-skinned, bespectacled manager of the basketball team, was crossing both sets of fingers under his desk, Haley noticed. "And you, Mr. Smithwick. Clearly, you had only a vague awareness of what this assignment was about," she said sternly. "I imagine your work will continue to slide once basketball season commences?" Dale closed his eyes before the C- paper landed on his desk.

Spencer Eton yawned as Ms. Lipsky approached his desk. "Mr. Eton, if you are going to try and pass off a previous work as a new paper, at least have the decency to change the date and header next to your byline." She placed in front of him a paper with the words *Eton, Freshman English* circled in bright red and a D! scrawled at the top of the title page.

"Oops," said Spencer with a smirk. "Then again, what have I got to worry about? My mom's running for governor."

"She hasn't been elected yet," Ms. Lipsky countered. "Now, Ms. Miller," she added, casting a long look in Haley's direction.

Every muscle in Haley's body tensed in preparation for the assault. *I knew I should have picked a stronger subject,* she thought, in full panic mode. *I did so well on the last paper, now she has higher expectations! My thesis was invalid! My argument was too literal! I cited all the wrong passages! She hated it! I just know it!*

"Nice work" was all Ms. Lipsky said as she dropped an A, Haley's second one in a row, and for the second time the only A in the class, onto Haley's lap.

Haley was stunned, though not so much so that she didn't notice the envious and annoyed glances bouncing around the classroom, aimed mostly at her. She tucked her paper into her backpack without bothering to read Ms. Lipsky's notes as a crackle came over the loudspeaker. Then came the all-too-familiar sound of Principal Crum's voice.

"Students. This is a reminder that tomorrow is picture day. So please, no purple mohawks overnight." Haley couldn't help but notice that Ms. Lipsky seemed to be hanging on Principal Crum's every word. She stared up at the intercom adoringly. "Dress like the men, ahem, or women you would like to become, and you will become those men. Eh, or women. Thank you, and good day."

Picture day! Haley thought, once again filled with anxiety.

Growing up with a father who was practically glued to a camera lens had made Haley more than a little uncomfortable about being filmed. She liked taking pictures of other people, but whenever the camera was turned on her, Haley stiffened up. So much so that she rarely came out looking like herself.

As the bell rang, she gathered up her things. "Congrats on the A, Miller," Annie said grudgingly as she and Dave passed by Haley's desk. "Guess it'll be stiff competition for class valedictorian."

"Annie, graduation is two and a half years away," Haley said, trying to soften the blow. She knew how much Annie cared about class rankings. "Besides, this was probably just a fluke."

"Two flukes in a row?" Annie asked skeptically. "I don't think so."

"But I don't even like to write," Haley added.

"Oh, great," Annie huffed, "so you mean to tell me you weren't even *trying*?"

"No—it's just—"

"Come on, Dave," Annie commanded. "We need to get started on our next term paper. Now. If Haley Miller can get an A from the Lipinator, so can we."

Dave shrugged in Haley's direction. "See you

tomorrow at picture day," he said, trailing off after Annie, and bumping into Sebastian Bodega on his way through the door.

Haley's fears about going in front of the camera were mounting by the minute. *The entire school will see this picture in the yearbook!* she thought. *I can't screw it up! I can't!*

"I wish I could take your picture right now," Sebastian said, closing one eye and framing Haley's face with his hands. "You look so . . . serious."

Haley snapped out of her daze. "Sebastian, what are you doing here?" she asked the hot Spanish exchange student.

"Ms. Lipsky is tutoring my English skills and helping me to write," he explained. "I spend my study breaks with her. Although if you would like this job, Haley, I am happy to change teachers."

"Sebastian, come now. Let's get started," Ms. Lipsky said, calling him over to her desk.

"You better go," Haley said. "She's a lot tougher than she looks."

"So I shall see you tomorrow with Dave and Annie for pictures, no?" Sebastian asked, squeezing her hand.

"Sure," Haley said. What she was thinking was, *Great. Another person to watch me make a fool of myself in front of the photographer.*

Haley forced a smile and waved as Sebastian followed Ms. Lipsky down the hall to the teachers' lounge.

"Hey, Haley," Reese said, sneaking up behind her once Sebastian had left the room. "I was hoping I'd catch you. I wanted to make sure you're coming to the game tonight."

Now that soccer season was over, Reese had moved on to his second-favorite sport, basketball. He was playing point guard on the Hawks' varsity basketball team. And tonight's game, Haley knew, was at home and against Hillsdale's biggest rival, Ridgewood.

In other words, it was not to be missed.

"Sure. I mean, I guess so," she said, wondering if staying out late at the game would mean dark circles under her eyes for picture day. *I certainly can't afford that*, she thought.

"Don't go to the game," Spencer whispered, vocalizing Haley's thoughts as he materialized at her side.

"And why not?" Reese asked.

"My parents are having this little fund-raising soiree at the house tonight. You know, a sort of kick-off before the actual kickoff of the campaign. Just some family, friends, insanely generous donors. Oh, and did I mention there will be an open bar?"

"That sounds like a great headline for your mom's platform," Reese said. "'Candidate Etons' underage son and friends get drunk at campaign fund-raiser.'"

"Lighten up, Natural Highland," Spencer said, before turning his attention to Haley. "You know you're always welcome at the Eton abode. Besides, it'll be a heck of a lot more fun than watching these guys get stomped by Ridgewood. Catch you later." He slung his backpack over his shoulder, put on his shades and wandered off down the hall.

"Don't mind him," Reese said. "He's just mad he didn't make the team this year."

"Gosh, I knew Spencer was bad at basketball, but I didn't think he was *that* bad."

"It wasn't his playing that couldn't cut it," Reese said. "It was his grades."

Haley found herself sharing Ms. Lipsky's sentiments about Spencer Eton's wasted potential. *He's smarter than half the people in this class, and he's doing worse than all of us,* she thought.

"So where are you headed next period?" Reese asked.

"Um, actually," Haley said, "I have geometry. . . ."

"Let me guess. You still get lost in the math wing?" he asked, picking up Haley's books and offering to walk her to class. "Don't worry. I know a shortcut. At least I think it's a shortcut. You do have your cell phone with you, right?"

● ● ●

Well, isn't Haley Miller suddenly Miss Popularity? At last count, she'd received three different invitations from three very different boys: a Latin hottie, a preppy bad boy and the adorable heartthrob-next-door. But which one will she accept?

To keep Haley close to Reese, turn to page 74. To take Spencer up on his invitation, flip to page 82. If you want Haley to spend time with Sebastian, Annie and Dave, send her to page 93. Finally, if you think it's most important for Haley to concentrate on her look before going in front of the camera, make her go home on page 69 instead.

Haley's clearly sailing through her classes at the moment, so she can afford to take a few breaks now and then. She'll either choose to spend that time wisely, or she'll . . . well, sometimes girls just wanna have fun.

WORKING TITLE

If only all of life's mistakes ended up on the cutting room floor.

Haley was having a hard time deciding on a format for her next big project. For starters, she needed an A just to survive the class. Until recently, art with Mr. Von, or Rick Von Wrinkle as he was known among his students, had been a slide. Nearly everyone got As.

But then Principal Crum had stepped in. Just before the holidays, the principal had met with the school board regarding some of Hillsdale High's "slacker" teachers. Then he had scheduled sit-downs with a few of the biggest offenders. Ever since then, Mr. Von had been a, shall we say, much tougher art critic. These days, he was handing out more Ds and Fs in art than Haley saw passed around in her advanced geometry class.

Haley wasn't just worried about preserving her perfect GPA. There was another incentive for doing well on the assignment. She also wanted to impress her artistically gifted friends.

It was difficult for Haley being around such art stars all the time. Shaun and Irene were practically young Picassos-in-training. They could draw anything upside down with their eyes closed. And Devon was an award-winning photographer at age seventeen.

Haley wanted to prove that she, too, had talent, to her friends but mostly to herself. So, each day after school, she sat in her room struggling to come up with a dazzling idea that would showcase her aesthetic strengths, whatever they might be. The problem was, in so many mediums, Haley had already bombed.

She had tried oil painting. Her canvases came out looking like oil slicks. With pastels, more chalk ended up on Haley's fingertips than on her blurry cityscapes. And her acrylics usually ended up bumpy and three dimensional, since Haley was constantly covering up her mistakes and starting all over again. Her watercolors were muddy and gray. She couldn't sculpt. She couldn't etch. And she certainly couldn't glaze ceramics.

Never in Haley's academic career had she been so entirely inept in a class. *I can solve quadratic equations in my sleep and I can't do* this? she thought, exasperated.

On a day when she was feeling particularly low, Haley wandered into the Millers' kitchen. Her grandmother—who had decided to stay on for a few weeks, at least until Joan's work schedule eased up—was baking chocolate chip cookies. Haley climbed up on a stool and let out a dramatic sigh.

"Okay, I'll bite. What's eating at my little dumpling?" Gam said, putting another tray of cookies in the oven.

"I'll never be a great artist," Haley said, laying her head down on the countertop.

"And you're just now figuring this out?" Gam said, motioning to a framed drawing Haley had done in the third grade. Even as an elementary school student, Haley's artistic inability had been painfully obvious. It was hard to tell if her subjects were stick people, buildings or trees. And the pallete, which was all dark browns and mustard yellows, wasn't exactly appealing either. "You get that from me, I'm afraid," Gam added. "To this day, I can't even draw a daisy. I'm like the opposite of Georgia O'Keeffe."

"So you're saying it's genetic. I'm doomed. There's no hope for me," Haley said, sinking further into despair.

"No, honey," Gam replied. "I came to grips with the fact that I can't paint or draw or sculpt a long time ago, but I still managed to find something else I can do, and do very well if I do say so myself."

"You mean . . ."

"I learned to knit."

Haley had to admit, even though Gam's knitted creations were at times embarrassing to wear, each stitch was beautifully and intricately produced. Her work, in its own way, was occasionally even as impressive as Shaun's, Devon's or Irene's.

"No offense, Gam, but I don't think I could learn to knit in time to get an A on my art project," Haley said, biting into a warm, gooey cookie and taking a sip from the glass of milk her grandmother had just set in front of her.

"Well, of course not," Gam said. "You have to find that something special that only Haley Miller can do." Gam paused and glanced over at the digital video camera Haley had recently gotten from her father as a Christmas gift. Haley instantly got the hint.

"But no one's ever submitted a film in art class before," Haley objected. "I don't even think it's allowed."

"There's a first time for everything, dear," Gam said as Haley reached for the camera, turned it on and watched some of the footage she had already filmed. She had to admit, the composition wasn't bad. She had a way of gracefully following a subject to fill out the frame.

"I'll even help you if you want," Gam offered.

"Okay, then. You'll be the Thelma Schoonmaker to my Scorcese. The Verna Fields to my Spielberg," Haley said, planting a peck on Gam's cheek.

"I was thinking more about feeding your crew for you, but honey, whatever you need me to do, I'm happy to help."

At that, Haley headed upstairs to plan her first feature film. Upon reaching her bedroom door, she found a list of phone messages in her father's handwriting tacked to her bulletin board.

Hi sweets. Annie Armstrong called to remind you about picture day this week. Irene Chen wants you to meet her at Hap's for dinner tomorrow night—something about preventing Shaun from ruining his life with that quest to become a professional eater? And last, but certainly not least, neighbor Reese wants to know if you're going to the first home basketball game this week. Since when did my little girl get to be so popular? Love, Daddy

Haley smiled fondly at the note. It was the first communication from her father in almost a week. Ever since Haley's mom had buried herself in a giant toxic torts case, Perry had basically been living at his office at Columbia. Even when he was home, he stayed locked in his study.

Joan was hardly any better. Haley had seen her only twice since Christmas Day. Her mom seemed to spend every waking hour at work, and came home only to shower and crash for a few hours each night.

The strain, Haley could tell, was getting to be too much on both of her parents. It was also beginning to affect little Mitchell, who was mimicking his father and spending more and more time alone in his room. Even Gam was having trouble luring him out with her cookies.

As Haley opened up a crisp new notebook and

began jotting down ideas for her art film, she couldn't help but wonder if the project she should have been working on, the one that took precedence over everything else, was mending her bruised family.

Perhaps, she thought, *there's a way to do both.*

● ● ●

Between Haley's absentee parents and Mr. Von's heightened scrutiny in art class, things aren't exactly rosy for Haley Miller at the moment.

What will happen to Haley's family in the coming weeks? Will her mother win her case? Will Joan and Perry be able to rekindle their love light once the verdict is handed down? And what about little Mitchell? Is he getting better or worse?

To keep Haley close to home, so that she can help out with Mitchell and figure out what's going on with her mom and dad, turn to page 69. To join Irene, Devon and Shaun at Hap's, where Shaun will attempt to eat his way into the record books, turn to page 100. To have Haley watch hot neighbor Reese Highland play in the first basketball game of the season, turn to HAWKS HUSTLE on page 74. Finally, hook up with Annie, Dave and Sebastian at PICTURE DAY on page 93.

Even though everything isn't coming up roses at the moment for Haley, with a little luck and some careful attention, she just might be able to coax her family tree to grow.

Nothing says home like the scent of home cooking.

In her first week back to school after winter break, Haley felt reinvigorated. Not since California had she been so focused on her schoolwork. Maybe it was the brisk East Coast air, or maybe it was all that positive reinforcement on her report card, but whatever the reason, Haley Miller was finally back to her over-achieving self.

On school nights, she stayed up late to finish, check and double-check her homework. She took on extracredit assignments, and was actually studying in study hall. With each new challenge a teacher threw at her came a hunger for more: more problems to solve, more facts to learn, more mysteries of the world to unravel.

Great book, Haley thought upon finishing a chapter of *Brave New World,* which was currently assigned reading for her honors English class. She placed the novel down on her bedside table and hopped up to her feet, feeling that light spring in her step that usually came after a particularly satisfying read.

Quite to Haley's surprise, going to public school was turning out to be a much more rewarding experience academically than she had ever expected. And for once, Haley was happy to admit she'd been wrong.

You know, school is just what you make of it, Haley thought, recalling a few kids at her old school in San Francisco who rarely studied and didn't much benefit from their teachers' constant praise and attention.

Then there were the public school prodigies—like Annie Armstrong and Dave Metzger—who wouldn't let little things like a lack of funding and overcrowded classrooms stand in the way of an Ivy League acceptance letter.

Haley looked at her cell phone to check the time. *Wow, eight o'clock,* she thought, peeking through her bedroom window and looking down at the driveway. Sure enough, neither of her parents' cars was there.

Why aren't they home yet? Haley wondered, exasperated. She found it inexcusable that Perry and Joan were working so late and, once again, hadn't bothered to call. *Guess we'll be eating without them for the sixth night in a row.*

The smell of Gam Polly's twice-baked cheesy potatoes wafted up the stairs and under Haley's door. Her stomach growled. As she made her way toward the stairs, she paused in front of her brother's room, then knocked on the door. "Hey, Mitch, how you doing in there?"

"You may. Enter," Mitchell said in his usual monotone. Haley nudged the door open and found him sitting on the floor in his pajamas, going through a stack of old family pictures. "I am. Starting. To forget. What they look like."

"Bet you're wondering where Mom and Dad are again tonight," Haley said.

"They fell. Down. A black hole."

"Well, not quite, buddy," Haley said, patting him on the back. "I know it's hard to believe, but you and me, we're very lucky to have parents who care so much about their work. A lot of people get stuck doing jobs they hate. And not only do our parents love their jobs, but they're making the world a little bit better place to live."

"I still. Would like. To see them sometimes."

"Tell you what, buddy. I'll make you a deal. If Mom and Dad aren't both home for dinner tomorrow night, I'll find out what's going on. Okay?" Mitchell nodded. "Now why don't we go downstairs and see what amazing feast Gam Polly has cooked up for supper?"

After devouring their "cheesy pots," turkey burgers and salads, Gam and Mitchell snuggled up on the couch in Perry's study to watch a DVD, while Haley returned to her room to perfect her look for the next day's class pictures.

Pictures, to Haley, were stressful business. Sure, she loved taking them. It was being on the *other* side of the camera that freaked her out.

As such, she needed to make sure she looked her absolute best, so that the potential for a disastrous photo—to be forever preserved in *That Talon,* the Hillsdale Hawks' yearbook—would be minimized.

Haley sat down in front of the mirror and began to experiment.

● ● ●

It's hard to say how wearing makeup will change Haley's image. Will it: a) make her look more grown-up; b) make her act more grown-up; c) make her feel more grown-up; or d) none of the above?

You get to tell Haley how to put her face on.

If you think she should give herself an alternative edge, have her put on coal black eyeliner to express her artistic side on page 132.

Stay soft and neutral with a pale pink blush and tinted lip gloss on page 105.

Go to page 120 if you think Haley should try a bolder look with mascara and berry red lipstick.

Finally, if you think Haley should skip the frivolous makeup, and want her naturally pretty face to shine through, have her dab on some clear lip balm and go au naturel on page 126.

Haley's fate from here on will be based on the way you've made her up. So you better hope you haven't transformed her into someone or something she's not.

A great three-point jump shot doesn't necessarily score points with parents.

What does she think, I have no life? Haley thought resentfully, pacing over to the front window to see if her mother was home yet. She stared at the empty driveway and shook her head. *Guess she's too busy to remember I had plans tonight,* Haley moped, recalling fondly the days when she actually had a mother.

Haley waited. And waited. And waited some more.

Finally, at a quarter to eight, her dad showed up and drove her to the basketball game.

In the car on the way over, Perry tried to make

excuses for why Joan had forgotten to pick Haley up. In doing so, he only made things worse.

"I don't care if she does win her case and it saves all of New Jersey from polluters," Haley seethed. "Do you know Mitchell told me the other day he's started to forget what you guys look like?"

Haley's father hung his head. "It'll get better soon, Haley. I promise."

"It better" was all she said before getting out of the car.

Once Haley entered the packed gymnasium, her mood began to lighten. The crowd was cheering hard for the Hawks, and Haley caught sight of Reese in his uniform, dribbling the ball down the court.

Haley looked at the scoreboard and saw that it was a close game. The Hawks were down by two, and it was already well into the second half.

A buzzer rang, signaling a time-out, and Reese Highland, Drew Napolitano and Johnny Lane jogged over to the bench drenched in sweat. The coach talked strategy to the winded, thirsty-looking starters as the team's manager, Dale Smithwick, refilled water bottles.

Haley scanned the home team bleachers. Annie Armstrong, Dave Metzger and Hannah Moss were seated behind Dale's spot on the bench, presumably so that Annie could continue her recent quest to pair off Hannah and Dale. Annie didn't like the idea of her own boyfriend, Dave Metzger, getting any closer to Hannah than he already was. Haley could just imagine Annie nosily leaning over Dale's shoulder as he tallied up stats in the official game book, and bombarding him with all of Hannah's "ah-mazingly" attractive qualities.

"Haley! Up here," Cecily Watson yelled, waving for Haley to come up and join her a few seats away. She looked radiant in a pale green cashmere sweater with jeans and boots, and, as usual, had a huge smile on her face. Haley climbed into the stands and sat down between Cecily and Sasha Lewis, who was wearing a fringed suede jacket and white tank top with her jeans. "You missed it," Sasha said wistfully. "Reese had a great first half."

"I can't even talk about it," said Haley. "My mom was supposed to drive me to the game, and she totally flaked."

"Well, at least you made it in time to watch the end of the game," Cecily said, trying to cheer Haley up.

The buzzer signaled again, and the players jogged back onto the court. Drew passed the ball to Reese, who dribbled to the key. Haley's stomach tensed. It made her nervous to see him playing in the Hawks' blue and gold uniform in such a close game. The stakes were definitely way up compared to pickup games in the Highlands' driveway.

Reese demonstrated exceptional ball-handling skills as he faked right and passed to the shooting guard on his left. Haley couldn't help but notice his defined tricep muscles.

"C'mon, guys!" Sasha hollered from the stands.

The shooting guard passed inside to Johnny Lane, who posted up his defender. He slapped the ball, pump-faked and went up for the shot.

"Foul, ref!" Sasha called out, jumping to her feet. "That's blatant contact!"

The whistle blew. The official in black and white stripes jogged over and stood directly in front of Dale and the scorekeeper's table. Putting two fingers up, he confirmed the foul was on number eleven from the visiting team.

"Come on, Johnny! Make those free throws," Haley cheered.

The three girls brought their hands up in solidarity and wiggled their fingers.

"Just like penalty kicks," Sasha said as Haley nodded in agreement.

Johnny stepped up to the foul line. He lifted his jersey to wipe the sweat from his brow and revealed his washboard stomach and tattoo of two tropical flowers.

"Johnny has a tattoo?" Cecily gasped, turning to Sasha for immediate answers.

"Oh, he has way more than one," Sasha said knowingly.

Johnny swished the first shot.

"Another one just like that," Sasha cheered, continuing the superstitious wave of her fingers.

Johnny made the second point.

"Nice!" Sasha called out.

Drew dribbled halfway down the court and passed the ball to Reese. Johnny, being careful not to foul, fended off two of Ridgewood's guards as Reese headed toward the basket with four seconds left to score. He planted his left foot to build some momentum, transferred to his right, ascended into a layup and . . . hit the game-winning shot just as the buzzer sounded.

The Hillsdale crowd erupted. Haley jumped to her feet, and she and Sasha and Cecily raced to the floor to congratulate their boys. The crowd quickly enveloped them. Haley found herself separated from Cecily and Sasha, and without a clue as to where Reese might be.

Suddenly, a moist hand reached out and grabbed hers. "Reese!" Haley said, wrapping her arms around him in spite of his sweaty uniform.

"I was worried you weren't going to make it," he said, kissing her on the forehead. "You're my good luck charm."

"It's a long story," Haley said. "I'm just glad I made it here in time to see that last play. You were amazing!"

"Ah, we're just having fun out there. Wait for me in the hall? I just have to shower off."

Haley waited with Sasha and Cecily for the boys to change. "Guess Coco and Whitney decided the Etons' fund-raiser was more important than supporting the home team," Haley said, shrugging her shoulders.

"Speaking of, have you guys noticed the gear

Whitney Klein has been busting out lately?" Cecily asked. "The other day, she showed up to study hall wearing a mink jacket over a leather bustier. That must be some serious guilt her parents are feeling over their divorce."

"Oh, I don't think Whitney's new wardrobe is coming from her parents," Sasha said knowingly. "In fact, I know it isn't. Her mother's flat broke, and Daddy Klein is too busy showering Trisha with gifts these days to pay any attention to Whitney. Besides, he's totally still pissed about Whitney's 'back to school' credit card bill. I wouldn't be surprised if Whitney is entirely without plastic at the moment."

"So then how can she be doing so much shopping?" Haley asked.

"Don't tell me she's dating some sugar daddy," Cecily gasped. "I knew she was into silver foxes, but I never thought she'd *act* on that impulse."

Sasha looked around to make sure no one was listening in. "Have you guys heard about the shoplifting plague in Bergen County?"

"Oh, yeah," Cecily said. "I heard we're supposed to have some sort of assembly about it."

"Ugh, does that mean we have to endure another one of Crum Bum's litanies?" Sasha wondered aloud.

"You don't think Whitney would've actually stolen anything, do you?" Haley asked Sasha.

"Oh, I *know* she would've," Sasha said without blinking. "You don't quit a shopping habit like hers cold turkey without some serious intervention."

Haley wondered if Whitney was even capable of theft on such a grand scale. This was, after all, Whitney Klein, the same girl who couldn't figure out the automatic lighter on her dad's gas stove.

The boys emerged from the locker room with combed wet hair and huge victory smiles. Reese took Haley by the hand. "Who's ready for some Hap's?" Drew asked, throwing his arm around Cecily. And with that, the six of them headed toward the parking lot.

● ● ●

Apparently, Sasha's competitive streak is at work even when she's not on the field. Just look at the way she was heckling that ref when Johnny Lane got fouled. And she wasn't exactly being magnanimous when she started talking smack about frenemy Whitney Klein.

Is Sasha in danger of becoming a mean girl, now that her popularity has been restored? Will the new Sasha-Cecily-Haley trio pick up where Coco and Whitney left off? Or are they too smart/cool to turn into queen bees?

What about Whitney? Do you think she's behind the recent shoplifting problem in Bergen County? If so, will she be able to get help before she gets caught?

It looks as though Annie Armstrong is still being shadowboxed by the unassuming Hannah Moss. Last semester, Hannah seemed to be going after Annie's boyfriend, Dave Metzger, with the full-court press. Will Annie be able to hold on to her man by pawning

Hannah off on the Hawks' manager, Dale Smithwick? Or is Hannah destined to become Annie and Dave's third wheel?

If you think there are no other girls Haley would rather be teamed up with, have her continue to hang out with Cecily and Sasha by turning to page 105.

If you're curious about what Annie was whispering in Dale's ear and think Haley should head to the yearbook committee to find out, go to page 126.

If it's social scandal and crime that really piques your interest, send Haley to find out what Principal Crum is torturing the students over now on page 111.

At this point, Haley could easily assume a spot atop the sophomore class heap—that is, if she wants it. With Sasha and Cecily as her BFFs, and Reese on her arm, Coco and Whitney don't stand a chance.

Unless you're the one with the funds, fund-raisers aren't all that entertaining.

On the night of the Eton fund-raiser, Haley received a barrage of text messages from Coco De Clerq. Coco claimed it was mandatory for all of Spencer's friends "to show face" at the event, whether they wanted to or not.

Haley had been looking forward to seeing Reese Highland play in the first home basketball game of the season. But she knew there would be plenty of other games to watch, and this might be her one and only opportunity to attend a campaign event for Mrs. Eton and see the curtain pulled back on Bergen

County's upper crust. After all, it wasn't every day that a friend's mother ran for governor of New Jersey.

"This looks pretty official," Perry Miller said as he dropped Haley off at the Etons' three-story stone abode, which was on one of the highest streets in Hillsdale Heights. Campaign signs were posted on the front lawn, and there were half-moon red, white and blue banners hanging from the eaves. New Jersey's state flag was strung up the flagpole, right next to the ol' Stars and Stripes.

A fleet of shiny black town cars surrounded the residence. The drivers all waited stoically behind partially tinted glass.

What if I'm not dressed appropriately, Haley wondered as she watched an elegant, suited couple stroll up the pathway to the house.

Haley looked down at her basic black V-neck sweater and striped trousers and frowned. "I'm sure Spencer will appreciate your being here," her dad said. "No matter what you're wearing."

Clearly, you don't know Spencer, Haley thought, smiling at her father. *And actually, we should probably keep it that way.*

"I'll see you at ten-thirty," Haley said, jumping out of the Millers' hybrid SUV.

Guess Coco and Whitney were right, running for governor does demand a few home improvements, Haley thought, noting the repaved driveway and slate-and-flagstone walkway that had been redone since Spencer hosted the last SIGMA.

Haley had overheard Coco and Whitney gossiping about the Etons in Spanish class earlier that week. According to their sources, Mrs. Eton had told Spencer, who told Ali, who told Coco, who told Whitney, who told the entire school, that for the past two weeks the house had been commandeered by the political outreach firm that was handling the event.

I wonder if Spencer's also gotten a gubernatorial makeover, Haley thought as she straightened her posture and rang the doorbell.

"Good evening," a lean butler greeted Haley. "May I take your coat?"

"Oh yes, sir, thank you," Haley said, prompting him to gently peel the coat off her back. He handed her a claim ticket. Haley walked into the parlor, which was abuzz with conversation.

"Would you care for white tea on ice or a red currant spritzer?" a woman carrying a silver tray asked politely.

Haley examined the fancy-looking drinks. "Hmmmmmmmm," she said, lingering over her options. The white iced tea was served in a frosted wineglass with crushed mint leaves, while the red currant spritzer came in a martini glass with a thin slice of orange on top.

"Thanks," Haley said, accepting a spritzer. She decided to take a lap through the crowd.

Oh, what's his name, Haley thought, trying to recall the name of an actor from one of her mother's favorite legal dramas. Joan had never missed an episode—that is, before she'd taken on the biggest case of her career and gone completely MIA.

Haley turned to her right and recognized another familiar face.

"Judge Ellis?" Haley blurted out, interrupting the gray-haired man's conversation.

"Yes, young lady?" the judge replied slowly, in an annoyed tone. "May I help you?"

"It's just that, my mother's arguing a case before you," Haley explained. "At least I think she is. I wouldn't know, really. You're probably seeing more of her than I am these days."

"Judging by your . . . hair color, and . . . blunt manner, I assume you belong to Joan Frasier Miller?" the judge asked, looking down at Haley over the rim of his spectacles.

"Um, yes, sir," Haley acknowledged.

"Right. Well, Ms. Miller, I would love to stay and hear what I'm sure is a scintillating story about how a young woman such as *yourself* came to be *here* in the Etons' home tonight. But I am afraid I am prohibited from interacting with the progeny of an attorney arguing a case in my courtroom before and during a trial, though not, unfortunately, after it. So if you'll excuse me . . ."

"Of course," Haley said, letting him pass. "Jerk," she muttered under her breath once she thought he was out of earshot. When Haley suddenly realized Judge Ellis had heard her, her eyes grew to the size of saucers and she fled in the opposite direction.

In the dining room, Haley wasn't at all surprised to see that Mr. and Mrs. De Clerq were monopolizing the Etons' attention. "Alison has applied to Yale," Maurice said proudly, putting his arm around his first-born daughter. "She's always been the brightest one in the family." Ali, who was standing somewhat dutifully at her parents' side, seemed to be stifling a yawn.

Where's Coco? Haley wondered. *And since when did the De Clerqs even realize they had another daughter, much less sing Ali's praises to other adults?*

"You know that Yale is my alma mater." Mrs. Eton smiled and turned to her husband. "We've always rather hoped Spencer would end up there."

"Say, wouldn't it be nice if Spencer and Ali found themselves at Yale *together*?" Mrs. De Clerq said suggestively.

"First I have to get in," Ali said, faking a smile and downing a swig of her spritzer.

"Admission is pretty tough these days," Mr. De Clerq added, trying to gloss over his daughter's somewhat sarcastic comment. "But our Ali, she's a smart girl. I'm sure she won't have any trouble."

"Well, you just let us know if you need any recommendations," Mr. Eton offered. "We have some good friends on the admissions board."

"We'd *really* appreciate that," Mrs. De Clerq said, patting Mrs. Eton on the arm. "And likewise, you let us know if there's anything we can do to help with the campaign."

"Anything at all," Maurice chimed in.

Just as Haley was about to make her approach and greet the De Clerqs and congratulate Mrs. Eton, she saw Coco motioning dramatically for her to come join her in the kitchen.

"Who was that *fox* you were talking to?" Whitney asked as Haley slipped through the door.

"Who, that geezer Judge Ellis?" Haley asked, trying to recall anyone else at the party she might have spoken with before entering the kitchen.

"Judge Ellis." Whitney repeated the name wistfully. "He's so dreamy."

Haley couldn't help but notice that Whitney was wearing an especially nice red floral dress, which was currently appearing on the cover of a major women's fashion magazine. "That is a beautiful dress," she said.

"Ask her where she got it," Coco said pointedly. She and Whitney exchanged an odd look.

"I'm a really good shopper," Whitney explained. "You should come with me some—"

"I see you decided to skip the basketball game," Coco interrupted, giving Haley an approving nod.

"Well, you said it: 'A party for our future governor is way more important than watching some stupid jocks dribbling a ball down a court and trying to stuff it through some hoop,'" Haley reminded her.

"I can't believe Spencer's mom is running for governor," Whitney said. Haley watched as she picked up a pastry knife covered with frosting and started licking it. "I can't imagine what that job is like."

"You can't imagine what any job is like," Coco said dismissively.

"So where's Spencer?" Haley asked. "And if we're here to support him, why are we hiding out in the kitchen?"

"Because he doesn't know we're here," Whitney explained, taking another lick of frosting. "He didn't invite us. Not after that scene Coco pulled on New Year's."

"Whitney!" Coco said sternly.

"Yep, Spencer didn't invite us, and we couldn't go to the basketball game because Coco would've been laughed out of the stands. Do you know there's footage of that night up on the Internet?" Whitney continued unabated. "Anyway, that's why we asked you to come, Haley. We need you to trot your little self out there, circulate and give us updates on how the party's going. Oh, and most importantly, we need you to talk Spencer into forgetting about that little New Year's Eve episode and giving Coco a second chance."

"Whitney!" Coco screamed again, this time so loudly she startled one of the kitchen waiters. He stumbled and nearly knocked over a stack of plates before turning to glare at the girls.

"Sorry," Whitney whispered, half to appease the waiter and half to appease Coco.

"This is ridiculous," Haley fumed. "I can't believe I let myself get talked out of going to the first home game of the season!"

"Look, all you have to do is make a few laps through the party," Coco explained. "Locate Spencer, get a read on how he feels about me, see if we still have a chance together, and then you can go to your silly basketball game."

"Why can't Whitney do that?" Haley demanded.

"Because he'll see it coming. You, on the other hand, he won't suspect."

"Why not?" Haley asked skeptically.

"Because he doesn't even think we're friends."

"Coco once told him she thought you were TPFW. Too Pathetic For Words," Whitney chimed in.

"That's it. I'm outta here," Haley said, turning to leave.

"Haley, wait, I'm begging you," Coco pleaded, grabbing her arm. "Look, I know I haven't always treated people well. I know I've been . . . mean. But I get that now, and I'm trying to change. I really am trying to be a better person."

"Oh, by spying on Spencer from his kitchen, at a party to which you weren't even invited?" Haley asked.

"Haley, I just don't want to lose him," Coco said plaintively, without any pretext. Haley had never seen her friend so vulnerable. It was TPFW.

"All right, I guess I could do one lap through the

party," Haley conceded. "But that's it. Even if I can't find Spencer, I'm going to the game." She turned to head back out to the party.

"Ooh, ooh, ooh," Whitney spoke up, "see if you can find out anything else about Judge Ellis."

"I honestly don't think he's your type, Whitney," Haley said.

"Ooh, ooh, ooh, and can you find out who's contributed the most money to the campaign so far?" Whitney asked. "I think it's so amazing how you just ask for money, and people give it to you. Just like that."

"That, I do know," said Haley. "Remember that slightly . . . overweight kid Shaun, with the blond mullet? Who's in some of my classes? Gosh, that reminds me, I've got to get started filming my art project."

"You mean that guy who's always carrying around jugs of paint thinner?" Whitney asked.

"That's him," Haley said. "His parents, it turns out, are big supporters of two things: fine art and politics. They've raised or given millions to Mrs. Eton's campaign."

"Interesting," Coco said, narrowing her gaze. "Shaun, you say."

Haley could tell that Coco was going to have a difficult time overcoming her evil gene.

"Ooh, ooh, ooh," Whitney added, "one last thing. Can you grab me some of those chicken wings, the ones with the spicy Asian sauce?"

"Is there anything else that either of you need while I'm out trying to repair your reputations?" Haley added through gritted teeth.

Coco and Whitney, sensing her anger, silently shook their heads.

Haley pushed open the swing door forcefully and returned to the festive party in the Etons' parlor and dining room. She couldn't believe she had just agreed to go on a Coco-Whitney errand. But then she had to admit, now that the dynamic duo of Whitney Klein and Coco De Clerq was essentially powerless and cowering in the kitchen, they were almost, kinda, not quite, sorta cute.

● ● ●

What do you think? Have Coco and Whitney been permanently dethroned? Or will they be able to fight their way back to popular status at Hillsdale High? Are they, as Haley suspects, more appealing as average classmates? Or will their destinies always keep them a cut above?

Now that Coco's fallen from grace, do you think she stands a chance with Spencer? Or is he completely over her, and will he now fall for her sarcastic older sister, Ali, instead?

Coco's parents also seem to have begun to favor Ali over Coco. Will Ali finally blossom under their love? Or will her sarcastic tendencies sabotage any chance at success?

And what about quirky Shaun's parents turning out

to be major art lovers and political donors? Will Coco figure out how to use their clout to her advantage? How will this news affect Shaun's status at school?

Talk about complicated. In the political scene, it's hard to keep track of everyone's motives. One thing's for sure: Haley needs to start taking her own alliances more seriously.

If you think Haley should continue palling around with Coco and Whitney, go shopping with the girly girls on page 120.

If you think something strange is going on when Whitney can suddenly afford clothes that have a price tag bigger than a small car, turn to page 111.

Finally, if you believe Haley might be better off with the nonjudgmental Shaun and his crew, have her head home to work on her video project for art class on page 132.

Just as there are some politicians who shouldn't be trusted, there are friends who need almost constant monitoring. Is Haley really ready to take on something like that? Or are Coco and Whitney just too much of a headache?

PICTURE DAY

**Every picture tells a story,
but who said all those
stories were true?**

Haley had been dreading picture day all week. She *hated* going in front of the camera. No, *hate* wasn't strong enough a word. She loathed it, detested it, thought it was worse than eating liver mush and brussels sprouts while watching a public television fund-raising drive.

Contrary to popular assumption, having a film-maker for a father did not necessarily mean you learned how to pose. In fact, Haley's father's habit of turning even a routine trip to the grocery store into a photo op had, through the years, made her acutely aware of just how *un*photogenic she was.

Haley knew she wasn't an unattractive girl. But somewhere between the moment the camera button was pushed and the shutter narrowed to close, Haley went from hottie to nottie. Yearbook photos were particularly bad since there was, after all, only one shot to get it right.

In her kindergarten class photo, Haley was missing her two front teeth and had grape juice on her lapel. Third grade? Her eyes were closed. In sixth grade, the photographer snapped her midsneeze. And in ninth, Haley unwittingly showed up on picture day with a fever, looking like an inpatient from a malaria ward.

As much as she hoped her luck would improve in Hillsdale, Haley was realistic about her chances of success.

Which is exactly why she came to school that day prepared, with three different outfit choices and a jar of petroleum jelly, which she planned to spread on her teeth to help broaden her smile. She had read that was a trick of beauty pageant contestants.

Even though it wasn't raining, Haley brought a slicker and an umbrella, just in case. She certainly didn't want to have wet hair in her picture. That was how she'd ruined her eighth-grade yearbook photo.

As the clock ticked down to zero hour—or 11:30 a.m., the time allotted for sophomore-class pictures—

Haley looked around for Annie, Dave and Sebastian and a little moral support.

"Hey, guys," she said, finding them lounging on a couch in the library. *Figures. Where else would Dave and Annie be,* Haley thought. *It's like they can never be more than fifty feet away from books, at all times.*

Sebastian, the hot Spanish exchange student who was on loan to Hillsdale for the year, had his nose deep in an English manual. As Haley approached, he looked up and smiled. "You look good, just like the food for to eat," he said admiringly.

"Um, thanks," Haley replied, not quite sure how to take the botched compliment.

Sebastian had never been shy about his feelings for Haley. And while she certainly liked him back, she had never figured out how to handle his constant showering of affection. Particularly when other people were around.

"I didn't think you cared so much about getting your picture taken for the yearbook," Annie said, noticing Haley's careful makeup and the green cashmere sweater she had just changed into.

"It's a long story. I take terrible yearbook photos," Haley explained.

"Oh, is that all?" Annie said. "You shouldn't worry."

"What do you mean?" Haley asked.

"You're looking at the yearbook committee. Or at least the two ranking officers of the yearbook committee."

"You and Dave?"

"Yep," Annie replied. "Eight members of last year's committee were graduating seniors, so Dave and I are the only ones with any experience left. Which means we've got all the power. Pick your nose in the photo if you want to. We can switch it out for a better one later. In fact, we can switch out anything later. Anything at all."

"Well, well, well." Haley was startled by the sound of Coco De Clerq's voice. "Look who discovered cashmere." Haley spun around to find Coco and wingbabe Whitney Klein staring her down. They were dressed impeccably. Haley was fairly certain she'd seen Whitney's black polka-dotted dress on a celebrity spokesmodel on TV recently.

"What are they doing in here?" Dave whispered to Annie. "The library is our turf."

"Are you lost again, Coco?" Annie asked in a condescending tone, looking up from her book. "The caf-e-ter-i-a is that way," she added, pointing toward an exit.

Whitney gasped, unable to fathom Annie Armstrong standing up to Coco. But then, ever since that fantastically awful scene on New Year's Eve at Richie Huber's, it seemed as if *everyone* was standing up to Coco De Clerq.

"So Haley, where did *you* get a sweater like *that,* anyway?" Coco demanded.

"What do you mean?" Haley asked.

"Well," Coco began, "that's imported twelve-, no,

fifteen-gauge cashmere. And you're, I'm guessing, more like a *blend* kind of girl."

"Maybe she's that shoplifter the police are after," Whitney said, in a tone that sounded as though she was trying to seem casual.

"My mom gave me this sweater for Christmas," Haley said emphatically. "She always buys me something green. It's our little joke."

"Suuuure," Coco replied.

"So what's this about a shoplifter?" Haley asked without taking her eyes off Whitney and Coco.

"Someone's been stealing from the local boutiques," Annie explained, standing up and staring at Whitney. "Supposedly it's a Hillsdale High student. Someone who, say, doesn't like the smaller allowance she's getting these days, now that her parents have separated. Someone who just can't bear the thought of a life without, *gasp,* shopping."

"Or someone like a new student who's so desperate to fit in, she'll do anything to be accepted," Whitney said defensively.

"It *is* interesting," Coco butted in, "Haley Miller suddenly developing such expensive tastes."

"Well, kids, we'd love to stay and debate the provenance of Haley's sweater," Annie said, linking arms with Haley and Dave, "but we've got to run. See you at picture day. Remember, girls, smile for the photographer. You only get one shot." Annie glanced over at Dave with a smirk.

Uh-oh, Haley thought, *I know of at least two*

photos that are definitely being switched out in the yearbook. And I bet they won't be for better pictures.

Later that morning, just before it was Haley's turn to go in front of the camera, Sebastian pulled her aside.

"Haley, there is something I have been wanting to ask you," he said. "The Americans, they have the break of spring. For these days, I will go back to my country and visit my family. My parents, they want for to meet my American friends. I am wondering, you will come with me? The Annie and Dave, they have already say yes."

"Go to Spain?" Haley gulped. "For spring break? Wow. That's a big trip. We'd be together twenty-four/seven. With Annie and Dave."

"You do not have to give me answer now."

Good, Haley thought, *because I don't have an answer to give you. What are my parents going to say? Then again, given their current work schedules, will they even know I'm gone?*

"Next!" a short, stocky photo assistant called out. She grabbed the still-stunned Haley by the wrist, dragged her over to the chair and sat her down in front of the camera.

Haley stared straight ahead, zombie-like, while the photographer counted to three and pulled the trigger. A flash went off. And then it was done.

Haley rose from the chair instinctively. "That one must be special ed, poor thing," the assistant said to the photographer, who nodded in agreement. At that moment, Haley realized she had once again bombed her yearbook photo. Only this time, instead of moping, she smiled. Because this time, she had a backup plan. And their names were Annie Armstrong and Dave Metzger.

● ● ●

Well, that was a bombshell of an invitation to drop on Haley just before she had her picture taken. Luckily, she has some time to think about it before she says yes or no to a trip to Spain with Sebastian.

Meanwhile, the shoplifting bandit is working his—or her—way through Bergen County. Do you think Whitney's the culprit? And will she get help before she gets caught?

To help Annie even the score with Coco—and to keep Haley close to Sebastian—turn to page 126. Find out more about the shoplifter in PRINCIPAL CRUM'S LITANY on page 111. Or observe Whitney as she goes SHOPPING WITH THE GIRLS on page 120.

Maybe getting into trouble wouldn't be such a bad thing for Whitney to go through. But will Haley just sit around and watch?

There's a point when food just stops tasting good.

"You've got to say something to him," Irene said. She was glaring at Haley in the parking lot of Hap's Diner with her arms folded across her chest.

"Why me?" Haley asked. She hated it when Irene tried to bully her.

"Because Shaun is tired of hearing me complain about it, and someone's got to stop him."

Haley kicked a pebble. "Really, Irene, aren't there more important things for us to be worrying about right now, like our art projects? Which are, may I remind you, due in three weeks. Plus, Annie

Armstrong just tapped me to be on yearbook committee. How in the world am I going to get out of that? And what about all these shoplifting episodes around Hillsdale? Don't you think it's kind of amazing that no one's been caught yet?" Haley rattled off a few of her most pressing concerns. "Plus, I totally think I saw my friend Gretchen in a toothpaste commercial the other day. On national television! I mean, toothpaste. So. Weird."

"Haley!" Irene scolded.

"Right," Haley said, "Shaun. I just don't understand what the big deal is. So Shaun wants to enter a few eating contests. It's just a phase. He'll grow out of it. Eventually."

"Not before he grows out of his size-forty-eight jeans," Irene countered.

"That just means there'll be more of Shaun to . . . like."

"And what about when it starts to affect his health?" Irene asked. "Then how will you feel? If he keeps putting on weight like this, soon he'll be too big to exercise. And then he'll get even fatter. It's a vicious cycle."

"Look, if you're so worried about him, why don't you just talk to his mom and dad?"

"Because Shaun does whatever Shaun wants in that house," Irene said. "You know that. He's an only child with parents who think rules discourage artistic freedom."

"Fine," Haley said in an exasperated tone. "If I

promise to say something to him, will you please just come inside? We're going to miss the Hap's challenge!"

"See, this is exactly what I'm talking about. You and Devon keep encouraging him!" Irene protested as Haley dragged her through Hap's front door.

"Hot diggity hot dogs!" Shaun bellowed as the girls approached him. "Throat, clear a path, because my stomach's now accepting visitors."

Piled high in front of Shaun was an almost comical amount of food. There was a plateful of cheeseburgers. One stainless steel bin was filled with hot dogs and another with french fries. Three blenders were practically overflowing with milk shakes. And there were heaping sides of potato salad, macaroni and cheese and one of Shaun's personal favorites, collard greens.

Ew, Haley thought, totally fascinated.

Hap's was a Hillsdale institution, known most of all for its eating "challenge." Old Hap would come out of the kitchen, look you over and tell you how much he thought you could eat. If you finished the order on your own steam, you ate for free. If not, well, you paid for everything he sent your way.

A crowd was starting to form as Shaun prepared to dig in. Irene reluctantly plopped down in a booth and turned her back to Shaun, while Haley sat down next to Devon.

One of the waitresses leaned over to another and said, "That's the biggest Hap's challenge I ever laid eyes on, and I've been working here thirty-five years."

The other woman said, "Either Hap's trying to put that kid permanently out of commission, or he thinks this one's really got something special."

Irene glared at Haley across the diner. "What?" Haley mouthed.

"You promised," Irene mouthed back.

"Shaun, listen," Haley began futilely.

"You timing me, Dev?" Shaun asked, paying her no mind. Devon held up a stopwatch and nodded.

"You really don't have to eat all this food," Haley continued. "I mean, what is there to prove? We already know you've got a superhuman belly."

But Shaun was beyond reachable at this point. He had entered the zone, that almost frightening state of focus that normally preceded his eating binges.

Devon pressed the start button on the stopwatch as Shaun scarfed down the first hot dog, then dipped the bun in water and swallowed that too.

"I can't watch this," Irene said, getting up from the booth and storming out of the diner.

It occurred to Haley that she should follow Irene out the door to make a point, but she was too transfixed to move. Shaun was like some sort of highly evolved mechanism of epicurean destruction. At times, he seemingly didn't even have to chew.

As she watched him consume the spread and win the Hap's challenge in just under fifteen minutes, Haley began to understand Irene's point. Shaun was more than likely endangering his health with his competitive-eating obsession. And it would only get worse if he continued on this track.

Haley also knew that it would take more than just talk to dissuade Shaun from entering any more eating contests. She would have to find a way to distract him. But how?

● ● ●

Irene certainly seems adamant about saving Shaun from himself. But do you think this eating machine will be swayed? With Shaun and Irene in a tiff, how will that affect Haley's relationship with Devon? It seems as if they're hardly able to see each other these days.

To have Haley start working on her art project—and trying to figure out how to distract Shaun from his bingeing—turn to page 132.

To find out more about that shoplifter Haley mentioned, head to page 111.

Alternately, have Haley see what YEARBOOK COMMITTEE with Annie Armstrong is like on page 126.

It's not unusual for artists to use their bodies in their work. But is Shaun's eating obsession a grand statement about society? Or is he just downing comfort food to get over his unreciprocated crush on Irene?

CHANGING OF THE GUARD

Every season usually yields a new crop of popular people.

The following Monday, before school, Haley put on the new creamy blush and tinted lip gloss she had recently picked up at the local pharmacy and sailed down the stairs with a soft pink glow on the apples of her cheeks.

"I'm sure gonna miss you, Gam," Haley said as she hugged her grandmother goodbye in the kitchen.

Gam Polly had just announced she was going back home to Pennsylvania on the train. Originally, Gam had planned to stay through Haley's sixteenth birthday, but now she said she needed to get back home to take care of "things."

Haley knew her grandmother was just trying to force her parents to deal with each other, and their kids. As long as Gam was around to keep the household together, Joan and Perry could continue working ridiculous hours without paying any consequences.

Haley also had a sneaking suspicion those "things" her grandmother needed to take care of back in Pennsylvania had something to do with a back-gammon-playing octogenarian neighbor, and the fact that Haley's birthday doubled as Valentine's Day.

"A little something for your birthday," Gam Polly said as she slipped a tiny square box into Haley's coat pocket and gave her a peck on the cheek. "My mother gave it to me when I turned sixteen. Promise me you won't open it until the actual day?"

"I promise," Haley assured her. "But I *will* be tempted."

Just then, a car horn beeped outside.

"That's my ride. I love you, Gam," she said and dashed out to Mrs. Lewis's vintage silver sports car purring in the driveway.

"Bye for now," Gam Polly called from the porch, waving as Haley climbed into the backseat next to Cecily. "Look after Mitchell for me."

"Okay, this is officially the coolest car in the world," Haley said as she sunk into the black leather interior.

"I put it in storage when I moved back to Paris,"

Pascale Lewis said, patting the dashboard affectionately and smiling at Sasha. "She's dying to stretch her legs."

After a polite toot of the horn to wish Grandma bon voyage, Pascale revved the engine and zipped off down the street.

Moments later, when the girls pulled up in front of Hillsdale High, a crowd gathered around the car. Everyone looked in their direction as Cecily, Sasha and Haley emerged, walking three abreast toward the main entrance of the school.

Haley couldn't help but notice they were garnering a lot of attention—stares, smiles, even pointing and whispering. *It must be the car,* Haley thought. *Or Sasha's ridiculously hot French mom.*

As they entered the school, necks craned to check out the girls. Sasha's flaxen locks were draped over her shoulders; Cecily's jet black mane was pulled up in a sleek ponytail; and Haley's long auburn bangs were stylishly tucked behind her ear.

Everyone who saw them seemed intrigued, even more so than usual. And this time, there was no denying it: The students weren't staring at the vintage car or Sasha's beautiful mother. They were staring at Haley, Sasha and Cecily, the sophomore class's new popular regime.

Wow, Haley thought. *This is sort of cool.*

"Freaky," Haley overheard Whitney say to Coco as the trio passed. "They've totally got the glow."

The former teen queens De Clerq and Klein were

huddled in a corner near their lockers trying to avoid eye contact, since they were both still embarrassed about Coco's bad behavior at Richie Huber's on New Year's Eve.

"Ladies," Spencer said as he swaggered toward Sasha, Cecily and Haley with Ali De Clerq at his side. "Ravishing, as always."

"Spencer," Coco called out when she spotted him, unable to help herself. "Did you get my messages?"

"Um, yeah," Spencer said, rolling his eyes. "Matt and I thought they were hilarious."

A varsity football player bumped into Coco and brushed by her. "Watch it, boys," he said. "She might hurl on you."

Coco's face turned scarlet. Haley felt momentarily sorry for her. "Um, Ali, I'll see you after school, right?" Coco asked nervously, desperate for someone to claim her.

"Oh, right," Ali said apologetically. "The 'rents want me to meet with my guidance counselor to see if there's anything else I need to do on my Yale app. Sorry, kid. I can't give you a ride home today. Mom and Dad thought you could take the bus."

"D'oh!" Spencer said, erupting in laughter and dragging Ali off down the hall.

"Wow," Cecily whispered to Haley and Sasha. "Did you *ever* think you'd see the day when Coco De Clerq would have to ride the *bus*?"

"What are you looking at?" Coco snapped at the

trio. "Whitney, my books." And with that, the deposed princesses slunk off to their next class.

"So, what do you guys have planned for the fourteenth?" Haley asked after the Coco-Whitney storm had passed.

"Johnny and I are just going to the music studio to practice," said Sasha. "You guys should stop by to hear my power chords," she added, warming up her air guitar.

"Hmmmm, a non-mushy, non-cheesy Valentine's Day activity that doesn't involve red hearts and balloons?" Haley said. "Count me in."

"Yeah, we can't *wait* to hear you rock out, Sash," Cecily said. "Wait, Haley, isn't Valentine's Day your birthday?"

"Okay, elephant memory," Haley said sheepishly, embarrassed to suddenly be the total center of attention.

"Why don't we make a night of it?" Sasha offered.

"Totally," said Cecily. "Drew would be into it. You know how much he loves the Hedon."

"And Reese said he wanted to see me after basketball practice," Haley added. "I'm sure he'd stop by."

"It's settled, then," said Sasha. "Here's to celebrating rock 'n' roll, Cupid and Haley's sweet sixteen!"

● ● ●

Well, the tables have certainly turned on Coco De Clerq and Whitney Klein since last semester. Dethroning the school's biggest queen bees wasn't as

difficult as everyone thought—all it took was a little vomit and a video camera.

But does Haley really want to be a part of the new ruling class? Or is the popularity game beneath her?

Sasha seems to have finally found her voice as a guitarist and singer in Johnny Lane's band. With each day, a little more of her healthy, natural radiance returns. But has she really learned all her lessons from past mistakes? Or are there still issues she needs to work out—namely, her father?

If you think that Haley, Cecily and Sasha have formed an alliance based on true friendship and common interests, have Haley spend her birthday with the girls and all their boyfriends on page 139.

If you suspect Haley, Cecily and Sasha have joined forces for the sake of furthering their popularity, have them test the limits of their emerging power on page 148.

If you don't think the idea of Haley spending her sixteenth birthday at a band practice is appealing, have her track down Coco and Whitney on Valentine's Day to see how the single girls live, on page 154.

Finally, if you think home is always where the heart is, send Haley home to blow out her sixteen candles on page 171.

Now that Sasha has discovered her passion for music, maybe Haley and Cecily will be the next to start pursuing their dreams.

The good things in life
aren't always free.

"Attention, students of Hillsdale," Principal Crum's voice crackled over the loudspeaker, jarring Haley from her careful virtual-dissecting work. "There will be a schoolwide assembly in the gymnasium immediately. I repeat, do not proceed to your normally scheduled classes. For those students currently on their lunch hour, we will find other times for you to eat. Please report to the gymnasium. We have a visitor here to address an urgent criminal situation."

The collective moans and groans of students

echoed throughout the hallways and corridors of Hillsdale High.

Is he kidding? Haley asked herself as the students from her honors biology class filed out of the classroom in an obedient herd. After five months at Hillsdale High, Haley had grown to expect the unexpected from the school administration, and, in particular, from Principal Crum. But now, she was beginning to understand the animosity that existed between the student body and the faculty.

"The school gods control your pea brains," the overweight cutup Shaun called out as he shoved his way down the hallway, pushing against the flow of the crowd. "My time is my money. My money is my time," said Shaun. "I will not be caged! Free the students. Free the students!" Haley watched as he slipped through an exit and escaped into the parking lot.

"I bet he's working on his next performance piece," Annie Armstrong said. Dave Metzger nodded in agreement a few feet in front of Haley. "I heard he's doing something big for Valentine's Day. As in, huge, gargantuan."

"Hey, what did you think of that digital pig fetus in lab?" Dave asked Annie.

"Ah! So realistic," Annie said enthusiastically. "I was working on the lymphatic system, and for a split second, I thought I had my hands on an actual pig!"

"You're telling me," Haley muttered under her breath. "I think it'll be a while before I eat another BLT."

"Oh, hi, Haley," Annie said, suddenly noticing Haley just behind them. "How've you been? I've been seeing so much of your mother lately because of this big Armstrong and White case, but I always forget to ask her about you."

"At least someone's been seeing her," Haley replied.

"Boy, is your mom a great dancer," Dave added, shaking his head and chuckling. "She's a wildcat."

Haley was getting angrier by the minute. Her mother didn't have time to come home for supper with her family because she was too busy *dancing* at the Armstrongs'?

"It's just to let off a little steam," Annie explained. "They take a ten-minute dance-party break every night at about ten, to get their energy levels back up. It totally works. They can usually keep on working through the night."

"Right," Haley said, rolling her eyes.

"Hey, isn't it almost your birthday?" Annie asked as they hit gridlock at the entrance to the gym. "So, do you have anything special planned yet? You can always do cake and ice cream at our place if you want to. That old coworker of your mother's from San Francisco, Peter Benson, makes a mean red velvet cake."

"I'll just bet," Haley said, unable to camouflage her annoyance as they slowly made their way through the gymnasium double doors. "Look, it's really nice of you to offer, Annie, but I need to find out what we have planned at home first. You know how parents like to make a big deal about the sweet sixteen thing. See ya." Haley forced a smile and began looking for a seat.

"Well, let us know if you reconsider," Annie called after her.

Haley glanced around the gym. Reese, Drew and Johnny had gotten their hands on a basketball and were shooting around competitively on the court. Johnny launched a comically enthusiastic shot from half-court and collapsed on the gym floor as Principal Crum entered with Officer Larchmont at his side. The duo, looking like Keystone Kops, marched over to the podium, stepping over Johnny along the way.

"Settle down, students," Principal Crum said sternly into the mike. "Silence in the gym!" he then commanded, pounding his fist against the podium. Finally, everyone began to take their seats and quiet down.

Haley sat down two rows above Annie and Dave.

"Guess Coco's approval rating is still in the toilet," Haley overheard Annie say to Dave as she motioned to where the former teen queens were sitting. They were surrounded by a ring of empty seats. "Trapped in social purgatory at last," Annie added, relishing Coco and Whitney's downfall. "Bad behavior always catches up to you."

Ever since Coco had gone on a drunken rant at Richie Huber's on New Year's Eve, and then thrown up on his bed and in his whirlpool tub, she had been a total outcast at Hillsdale High. As in, lower than the dweebs who spent their summers in band camp, and more ostracized than the thugs from the Floods. Whitney, because she continued to hang out with Coco, had been banished from the popular crowd as well.

Principal Crum cleared his throat. "For some of you, we are interrupting a science lab." He leaned a little too close to the mike and sent a blast of feedback through the loudspeakers. "Others will be missing a mathematics lesson today. For the unlucky few, this is your lunch period."

This last statement was received with harsh boos from the crowd.

"Relax, people," Principal Crum continued. "We will find time for you to eat. But first, why have we called you here today, I ask?"

My thoughts exactly, Haley thought, her stomach grumbling.

"Why am I holding yet another assembly out of the clear blue sky?" He paused for a moment and added, "Though I guess, technically, today the sky is neither clear nor blue."

"Damned if I know!" Chopper called out from somewhere in the upper bleachers. Haley recognized the voice, though Principal Crum clearly didn't.

"Who said that?" Crum demanded, furrowing his brow and gazing into the crowd. "So help me . . ."

Officer Larchmont coughed, and looked at Principal Crum impatiently.

"At the start of this year a vandal defaced our

school," Crum continued. "Shortly thereafter, a thief stole money from our cafeteria. In both of those cases, justice was served. But the problem we face today is a different kind of criminal-animal. This infraction will not lead to suspensions, detentions or services owed or rendered to our school. The crime we face today will be punishable by state law. Which is why I have upped our alert level to aubergine."

"Ooooooooooohhhhh," the students moaned in collective mock horror.

"Officer Larchmont," Principal Crum said in a booming voice, "I don't think my students realize the gravity of this situation. Would you mind expounding on this predicament for them?"

Officer Larchmont stepped up to the microphone. "Kids, this is a very serious matter. Over forty-five hundred dollars of merchandise has been lifted from Mimi's Boutique alone."

Haley recognized the name of the boutique where Coco and Whitney liked to shop. She glanced over at the ousted duo and noticed that Whitney had a pained expression on her face.

Officer Larchmont continued. "I have the entire Bergen County retail community calling for mandatory sentencing when the culprit—or culprits—is found. Even if he, she, is a minor."

Whitney looked ashen.

"Advanced surveillance systems are being installed at local businesses," Officer Larchmont said. "And I can assure you, the person or persons will be caught, and they will be punished to the fullest extent of the law."

"You heard Officer Larchmont. This is a crime of the utmost magnitude," Crum said as he returned to the podium and adjusted his pants, pulling them up high above his waist. "Now, I want you to think long and hard about the implications of this matter, and if you have any pertinent information, I urge you to come forward. Students, you are dismissed. You may return to your classes, unless you missed part of your lunch period, in which case you may proceed to the cafeteria."

The principal's last set of instructions caused an uproar. Everyone went straight to the cafeteria, regardless of when their scheduled lunch period was. The teachers didn't have time to check who belonged there and who didn't, and no one wanted to miss out on the fun.

The lunchroom was soon overloaded with triple the amount of students it could seat. The cafeteria ladies scrambled to shut down the buffet and lock the kitchen doors, for fear of students rioting over the only few sloppy joes and slices of pizza that remained.

Since there were still hungry students, someone with a cell phone called Lisa's Pizza and ordered a few dozen pies for delivery. A hat was passed to collect funds.

While waiting for the food to arrive, Haley wandered through the cafeteria, searching for any and all recognizable faces. She finally found Sasha Lewis,

Johnny Lane, Cecily Watson, Drew Napolitano and Reese Highland ensconced at a corner table.

Sasha spotted her too and waved Haley over.

"Hey," Sasha said. "We were just talking about you."

"Really?" Haley asked, somewhat surprised.

"How would you feel about joining us for our anti–Valentine's Day celebration at the studio?" Sasha asked, giving a quick look at Reese. "Cecily, Drew and Reese are all coming over to watch our band practice. Could be fun."

Haley had heard that Sasha had recently joined Johnny's band, the Hedon, as a guitarist and singer. "I'm sure it would be fun," Haley said. "The only thing is, February fourteenth is actually my birthday."

"Really?" Reese said, raising an eyebrow.

"Anyway, I've got to see what my mom and dad have planned. You know how parents can be about the whole sweet sixteen thing."

"Boy, do I ever," said Cecily. "My parents are already talking about what they want to do for mine and it's not until June."

"Oh, come on, Haley," Johnny coaxed, looking over at Reese and then back at her. "What could be better than hanging out with all of us on your birthday?"

Gee, I can't imagine, Haley thought, staring into Reese Highland's dreamy gaze.

"I bet I could even rustle up a cake," Reese said, smiling back at her.

Well, that was close. Haley's honors class schedule nearly doomed her to a home-baked birthday with the kids from her bio lab, Annie Armstrong and Dave Metzger, while Sasha and Cecily would have been off having fun with the boys.

So what do you think Haley should do for her birthday?

If you think Haley should celebrate her sixteenth with the rockers and rollers, head to the Hedon's band practice with Sasha, Johnny, Cecily, Drew and Reese on page 139.

To send her home to find out what her parents have planned, turn to page 171.

If you think Haley stands a better chance of seeing her absentee mother at the Armstrongs' house, take Annie up on her invitation on page 162.

Or, if you're curious about what Coco & Co. are up to on Valentine's Day, send Haley to celebrate her birthday with the Coco clique on page 154.

Finally, if you want to find out what the wacky Shaun has planned for his Valentine's Day performance art piece, go to page 178.

Haley will likely remember her sixteenth birthday for the rest of her life. What type of memory do you think she should have?

SHOPPING WITH THE GIRLS

It can be near impossible to keep habitually sticky fingers clean.

A selection of Top 40 music was blaring in Mimi's Boutique as Haley picked over the racks of clothing with Coco and Whitney.

"Wow, they have every designer I've never even heard of," Haley joked, holding a café latte in one hand and a brand-name bolero in the other.

"I know," Coco said earnestly. "This is my absolute *favorite* shop for all formal events, general retail therapy and ERO."

"What's ERO?" Haley asked.

"Emergency Reputation Overhaul," Whitney explained.

"Trust me, Haley," Coco said, "by the time we leave Mimi's this afternoon, we'll be brand-new women."

"And I take it that's a good thing?" Haley asked skeptically.

"Of course," said Whitney. "I mean, we've got to restore our rightful place at the center of the Hillsdale High universe, right? Because without us to worship, all those other kids are just like a shepherd without any sheep."

Coco shook her head and looked at Haley. "You get the point."

"Right," Haley said. "Those are really cute, Whitney," she added, admiring a pair of skinny jeans Whitney had just picked up.

"Cinched cropped is the new baggy layered," Whitney announced, looking left and right, then lifting up her skirt and wriggling into the jeans without bothering to go into a dressing room. "And, they fit. Perfect." Whitney pulled off the tags and put them with her stack of clothes, then went back to perusing the racks.

"Chastity is the new sexy for me," said Coco, picking up a turtleneck sweaterdress and adding it to her pile. "What would you guys think if I started volunteering at a soup kitchen? Would that convey committed, responsible and compassionate?"

"Um, sure," Haley said, watching Whitney as she obsessively examined the weave of a baby blue cashmere sweater. "It has a good hand," Whitney finally declared, using the fashion industry terminology she'd picked up at a trunk show in New York earlier that year.

"Wow, Whitney," said Haley, "I knew you liked clothes, but I had no idea you knew so much about fabric and construction."

"She *has* been competitively shopping since the third grade," Coco said.

"I'd spend every waking hour in here if I could," Whitney added. "School is such a bummer."

"Hey, what are you guys doing for Valentine's Day?" Haley asked. She still hadn't mentioned that the fourteenth of February was her sweet sixteen.

"Ugh, I don't know," Coco said, throwing herself down on an armchair. "Do you think I have time to revamp my entire life and make Spencer fall in love with me all over again?"

"*That* might be pushing it," Haley said.

"I think we should go out and have fun anyway," Whitney said. "Who cares if we don't have dates?"

"I do," said Coco. "If we go out, we risk other people seeing us alone on Valentine's Day. And that's an immediate social status reduction. Everyone knows that."

Haley pulled off her sweater, leaving only a tank top underneath, so that she could try on a blazer.

"Holy comoly," Whitney gasped. "When did you sprout those melons?" She and Coco gawked at Haley's C cups popping out of her tank top.

"Wait, did you get a boob job over the holidays?" Coco demanded.

"Only a natural one," Haley said with a frown. "They just don't seem to stop growing."

"Well, that blazer looks fantastic on you," Whitney said. "It emphasizes your curves while downplaying the vamp factor. You should totally get it."

"It does look . . . nice," Coco added. It took her a moment to realize what she'd just said. "Ohmigosh, you guys!" Coco shrieked. "I just gave Haley a compliment! And I *meant* it! I totally meant it! Maybe I really am changing!"

Coco dashed off to the dressing room to try on her finds, while Whitney and Haley proceeded to the register. Haley reluctantly took off the blazer and gave it back to the salesgirl. "I have to talk to my mom about it," she explained. "We have an agreement that I don't buy anything over a hundred dollars without consulting her, and she keeps giving me an allowance."

"That's a good plan," said the clerk.

Yeah, the only problem is, Haley thought, *I haven't laid eyes on the woman in almost a week. How am I supposed to ask my mom about a blazer when she's almost never home?*

"Well, I'll take everything," Whitney said, unloading her piles on the counter. Haley took out her video camera and hit the On switch as Whitney threw down her father's credit card, then made a series of pouty faces for the camera.

"I'm sorry, Jerry?" the store clerk said, handing back the card. "It didn't go through. Do you have another one I could try?"

"Not possible," Whitney said. "It's not even one of the accounts Daddy cut off when he got my back-to-school bill. This was my emergency-uses-only card. It's supposed to *always* work."

Coco appeared behind them. "Well, that red velvet dress definitely qualifies as an emergency. Do you want me to get it for you?"

Whitney shook her head. "I'll just put this stuff back."

"I can do it," the clerk said.

"That's okay," Whitney replied. "I want to spend a few more minutes with my babies before I put them up for adoption." She slinked back to the rack with her things and lovingly began returning some of the garments to their hangers.

"Can you wrap these up for me?" Coco said to the salesgirl, handing her a dozen different pieces. Coco then caught Haley's eye and dramatically added the word, "Please."

● ● ●

It looks as though Haley won't be wearing something new on her birthday. Not unless her mother has a psychic revelation about that blazer at Mimi's Boutique.

And given Joan's hectic work schedule, will she even re-member it's Haley's birthday at all?

Who knew there was a limit to Whitney Klein's credit line? Maybe Jerry has finally cut her off for good. If so, how will she cope? Will Whitney be able to handle leaving the store empty-handed?

What about Coco? Do you think she's really changed? Or is she just pretending to be nice until she regains her popular princess status at Hillsdale High?

Send Haley to find out who will get the most love and affection on Valentine's Day this year—Coco, Whitney or Haley—on page 154.

If you think Whitney and Coco are too "clothes-minded" for Haley, have her head home to see what her parents have planned for her birthday celebration on page 171.

Will Haley get any love and affection on Valentine's Day this year? Or will Cupid overlook her entirely? It all depends on how you choose.

YEARBOOK COMMITTEE

Everything looks better or worse in hindsight.

Haley watched as Annie Armstrong banged a gavel on a table at Drip, the local coffee shop. Annie was calling the Hillsdale High yearbook committee meeting to order. "Okay, people," Annie said, "first things first. What we need is a theme."

Despite the fact that Annie was only a sophomore, she had earned the title of yearbook committee chairwoman—a post that, Haley was learning, brought with it a startling amount of power.

Not only did the committee head get to choose the yearbook's annual theme, she also had control over every single quote, every phrase and, perhaps most importantly, every picture that was included in the tome. Nothing, absolutely nothing, went into the yearbook without Annie's approval.

Haley had signed up to help, partly out of curiosity, but also because she wanted to make sure the portrait of her that everyone from school would see wasn't too humiliating.

It had already been a tough enough few weeks, what with her mom pulling a disappearing act and staying late at the office every night, her dad locking himself in his study all the time to work on his documentary, and Sebastian always busy with either his English tutor or college swimming scouts.

Now, Gam Polly was leaving to go back to Pennsylvania. On practically the eve of Haley's sixteenth birthday. The fact that her birthday also fell on Valentine's Day, and that Haley's romantic life hadn't exactly been secure of late, pretty much meant that it was going to suck no matter who planned the festivities.

Haley had been waiting for Annie to offer to throw a party, or at the very least plan a dinner. Haley had, after all, gone out of her way to make sure Annie had a great birthday just a few months back. However, these days, all Annie seemed to care about was the yearbook.

Annie had made her constant companion, Dave Metzger, the committee secretary. Like Annie, Dave had been one of the only students with any previous yearbook committee experience to sign up. Aside from Annie, Dave and Haley, the committee basically consisted of a bunch of freshman girls who all seemed to hang on Annie's every word.

"Any ideas?" Annie said, looking around at her freshman admirers.

"How about 'the Time of Our Lives'?" one girl asked hesitantly.

"Do your research, Coleman," Annie said harshly. "That was Hillsdale High's theme in 1994."

"'This Is Our Youth'?" another freshman asked.

"Too obscure," Annie replied, looking down her nose at the girl. "Do you honestly think anyone in the senior class would get the reference? My cat has a higher IQ than the valedictorian."

Dave chuckled and shook his head. "That Lucas," he said, cracking himself up over Annie's cat. "You should see him with a ball of twine."

"What else have we got?" Annie asked. "I need to go to the printer with a theme by Monday, and I can't very well bring her any of this garbage."

"Annie, don't you think you're being a little . . . harsh?" Haley asked, butting in and sticking up for the freshman girls. "I mean, this is only a yearbook we're talking about."

"Only a yearbook!" Annie said incredulously. "Only a yearbook? You talk to me in twenty years, when this yearbook is your only memento of a simpler time, when all that mattered were your grades and whether or not you had a date to the next formal."

Wow, Haley thought. *Now I know what Mr. Tygert was talking about when he said "absolute power corrupts absolutely."*

"'Thanks for the Memories'?" a smiling girl with braces and long braids said, interrupting Annie's tirade. Little did she know she was about to get beaten down in response.

"I didn't ask for a theme our grandparents would like," Annie said dismissively. "Next!"

"'The Golden Years'?" another girl asked.

"Cecilia, what is it about the directive 'current' that you don't understand?" Annie demanded. "Because sometimes it feels like I'm talking to myself. Dave, an ibuprofen. I feel a headache coming on."

"Listen, why don't we all take a break from themes for a while and move on to pictures," Haley suggested, trying not to sound too eager.

"Fine," Annie said with an annoyed wave of her hand. "But I'm warning you, none of us is leaving this table until we have a working theme for the yearbook. Dave, the proofs."

Dave handed over the stacks of photos for each class. Haley nonchalantly shuffled through the pile until she located the *M* section of the sophomore class. She scanned until she came to her photo. Or rather, the place where her photo should have been. Instead, there was a blank spot with the name *Haley Miller* beneath it.

"Are you looking for *your* photo?" Annie asked.

"Trust me, you wouldn't have wanted to see it. I had them cut it out entirely. Just bring me a picture you like of yourself, and we'll slip that in instead."

"Really? Because—"

"Oh, no need to thank me, Haley," Annie said in a condescending tone. "I'm sure there will come a day when you can repay the favor."

I'll just bet, Haley thought, sensing that Annie was likely to call in that favor sooner rather than later.

"Hey, this doesn't look like Coco De Clerq," the girl with braces said, pointing to the place where there should have been a photo of Hillsdale High's most popular sophomore. "And that's definitely not Whitney Klein. Or at least it's not what she looks like now."

"Give me that!" Annie snapped, yanking the proof out of the girl's hand.

Haley caught just a glimpse of what looked to be heinous, no-makeup, alternate-universe-level photos of Coco and Whitney. *So, Annie's finally getting even after all these years they've tortured her,* Haley thought. *Guess they probably deserve it, after everything they've pulled.*

Somehow, though, as Annie smiled her Cheshire cat grin and clearly reveled in her revenge, Haley began to miss the old, sweet, lovable, if at times annoying Annie.

"Now, back to our theme," Annie barked.

The new Annie wasn't exactly easy to live with.

• • •

Wow, has Annie ever gone overboard. But is it a permanent change, or will the good-natured Annie eventually resurface?

To have Haley trust that her friends will pull through on her birthday, turn to page 162.

Or, if you've had enough of the new, empowered Annie Armstrong, send Haley home to see what her family has planned for her sweet sixteen on page 171.

Alternately, you can place Haley in the halls of Hillsdale High on Valentine's Day on page 154.

Love is in the air this February in Hillsdale. It's just a little unclear if any of it will be directed at Haley Miller.

The biggest pitfall with any narrative is losing the plot.

Haley could have sworn she had seen her old friend from San Francisco, Gretchen Waller, in a split-second flash of a toothpaste commercial during one of Gam Polly's cop drama shows. But she couldn't be sure.

Once the ad went into heavy rotation and began broadcasting, oh, like every five minutes on major network and cable stations, Haley realized she was right. It *was* Gretchen smiling that big cheesy grin and polishing her teeth with the aqua-colored toothpaste.

Haley IM'd Gretchen to let her know she'd seen

the spot. Gretchen IM'd her back, telling her about all her new acting projects, not just the commercial.

As luck would have it, Gretchen was planning to be in New York the following week, to audition for an off-Broadway play. She said she might even be able to come to Hillsdale for a few days, schedules permitting.

Haley was ecstatic. Since Gretchen, the actress, would be in Hillsdale . . . and Haley, the budding director, was planning to make a movie for her big art project . . . Haley wondered if she could ask her oldest and dearest friend to be the lead in her short film.

Where, after all, was she going to find a more talented or experienced thespian on such short notice?

Haley had already convinced her grandmother and Mitchell to participate in the project. With the prospect of Gretchen as her lead, she finally had an idea for a storyline.

Haley spent the following two days sketching out scenes and dialogue, and by the time Gretchen arrived, she had a working script.

"Thanks so much for doing this," Haley said as Gretchen, Gam and Mitchell climbed out of the Millers' hybrid SUV in the Palisades in full costume.

They were in a wooded section of the park, which looked a little eerie now that the leaves had all fallen. *Now I know what Dad means when he talks about deciduous trees being the great silent actors of nature,* Haley thought. *They really do convey the whole spectrum of human emotion.*

Gretchen had on a blond braided wig and a green and red pinafore over a stiff white blouse; Mitchell was wearing tiny green lederhosen; and Gam had on a long black dress with a cape.

"I'm just glad I could help out," said Gretchen.

"What. Do you want. Me. To do," Mitchell asked robotically.

"Mitch, buddy, you're playing a boy named Hansel. And guess what? Hansel doesn't talk like a robot. Do you think you can help me out and talk in a Hansel voice for a little while?"

"Sure, Haley. Why didn't you say so?" Mitchell said, speaking in plain English for the first time in recent memory.

Haley tried not to act surprised since she didn't want to spook him. "Great," she said, turning away so that he wouldn't see her massive grin.

"Well, I just think it's wonderful that you've decided to make a real action movie for your art class," Gam said, fussing over Haley. "You know your father was about your age when he first picked up a camera."

"Yeah, but Dad just pointed it at a tree and stood there," said Haley. "Okay, let's get started. Everyone remember his or her lines?"

Gretchen, Mitchell and Gam nodded. They spent the rest of that Saturday filming each scene in several takes so that Haley had a fair amount of material to use.

Back at home that night, from the moment she

saw the footage on her computer screen, Haley knew she had made something special. Gretchen and Mitchell interacted naturally, since they'd basically known each other their whole lives. Gam was charming and quirky in some scenes, and suitably spooky in others.

But the breakout star was Mitchell, who seemed to have a natural gift for acting. Or maybe Haley was just captivated because he wasn't speaking like a robot. In any case, Haley couldn't believe how *normal* he looked. Had her parents been speaking to each other, or even at home that day, she would have raced to their respective rooms to show them the new Mitchell.

As it was, Haley wasn't even sure when she would see them again.

"I'm so bummed I can't stay for your birthday," Gretchen said as she packed up to head back into the city for her audition.

Haley had nearly forgotten all about her birthday. But sure enough, it was almost February fourteenth.

"Ah, I've gotten used to not really celebrating," said Haley, trying to make Gretchen feel better. "It's not exactly easy to be born on Valentine's Day."

Gam Polly was also packing her bags, to return to Pennsylvania on the train just a few days before Haley's birthday. Gam had told Haley that she would've loved to stay, but as long as she was in Hillsdale, Joan and Perry could go on avoiding their problems and their children. It seemed as if leaving would probably be the best thing for everyone.

Haley knew, though, that Gam's rush to get back to Pennsylvania also had something to do with a certain backgammon-playing octogenarian neighbor, and the fact that Haley's birthday doubled as Valentine's Day. *Good for her,* Haley thought, admiring her spunky grandmother for having a dating life at the age of seventy-two.

Before she left, Gam gave Haley a small package not to be opened until the morning of her sweet sixteenth. With everyone out of the house, and Haley's modern take on a classic children's fable complete, she could concentrate on her parents and figuring out how to help Shaun and get him to drop his crazy obsession with eating contests.

Haley decided the best thing to do was just sit down with Shaun and talk things out face to face. So, the following Monday after school, she confronted him.

"You want to know what I think? I think you're overeating to substitute for something else in your life that you can't have," Haley said to Shaun as they sat on Devon's hood in the parking lot.

Shaun watched as Irene came out the front doors of the school and stopped to say hello to Johnny Lane, the hot rocker from the Hedon, whom Irene had had a crush on for years and who already had a girlfriend in Sasha Lewis.

Shaun's face lit up when he saw Irene, then fell as he watched her torture herself by talking to Johnny. "Hoss, you know me inside out."

"Eating is never going to make up for Irene," Haley continued.

"I just end up with broken heartburn."

"So, what are you going to do about it?" Haley asked.

"Shaun don't see no way out," he said. "Shaun thinks eating at least dulls the pain, while giving Shaun another gastrointestinal sort of pain."

"Why don't you just . . . go for it with her?" Haley suggested. "You'll never be sure unless you try. And who knows. People do change their minds."

They both watched as Irene hung on Johnny's every word.

"Not that much, hoss," Shaun said.

"Well, remember what I said," Haley advised as she headed back inside for her next class. "Go for it."

Shaun shook his head and said, "I just might."

● ● ●

Shaun's dormant passion for Irene seems to be serving as a rumbling in his tummy, making him scarf down everything in sight. Will he keep eating his way through greater Hillsdale? Or will he make a real bid to win Irene's heart this Valentine's Day, perhaps with a grand, dramatic gesture?

It looks as though Haley has finally figured out what she's good at. Clearly, she inherited Perry's filmmaker genes, along with Joan's courtroom flair for building suspense. It's just too bad Haley's parents aren't around to see their daughter finally coming into her own.

With Gam and Gretchen now gone, what do you think will happen on Haley's birthday? Will Cupid come to call? Will Shaun win over Irene? And will Haley's parents even remember what's significant about the day? Find out what happens with Shaun and Irene on page 178. If you'd rather see what Haley's parents have in store for her birthday, turn to page 171.

Even perfect families have bad days. Make that bad months. Joan and Perry are bound to snap out of it sooner or later. But will Haley be able to forgive them when they do?

BIRTHDAY AT BAND PRACTICE

Even the life of the party can flatline without good tunes.

Haley woke up on the fourteenth of February feeling remarkably content. She had already decided she wasn't going to let it bother her that her parents had forgotten about their only daughter's sweet sixteenth. Having her own plans for the night certainly helped. After all, compared to attending the Hedon's band practice with Reese, Johnny, Sasha, Drew and Cecily, Haley's old-fashioned cake-and-ice-cream birthdays with Mom and Dad now seemed quite quaint.

Haley spent the morning making a pancake breakfast for Mitchell. There was no birthday card waiting for her downstairs, just a note in her father's handwriting letting her know that Joan had pulled another all-nighter at Armstrong & White, and that Perry was already on his way to Columbia for an early-morning meeting with one of his students.

I can get angry and upset, or I can have a good time tonight on my own, Haley kept telling herself. *Besides, Mom and Dad will feel worse if they have to figure it out on their own.*

At least Mitchell hadn't forgotten. After breakfast, Haley opened his homemade present—an old flashlight with a cardboard snowflake attached. It cast shadows on the wall that looked a bit like falling snow.

"Wow, thanks, Mitch. I love it." Haley gave him a hug.

"What else. Did you. Get," Mitchell asked.

"Well . . . did you see the locket Gam left for me before she went back to Pennsylvania? Gam's mother gave it to her on her sweet sixteenth. And since Gam didn't have any daughters, it got passed down to me." She held up the platinum locket she had opened that morning in her room. It had a long oval shape, with some filigree and etching on the sides.

"That is. Very. Pretty," Mitchell said, mopping up the last bit of syrup on his plate with a forkful of pancakes.

"Thanks, buddy," Haley replied. "So you'll be okay at Henry's tonight? Are you sure you don't want me to cancel my plans and stay home with you?"

"Negative. Henry's mom. Is. Picking me up. From school. I will return. At oh-nine-hundred. On Satur. Day."

"Well, I'm so glad you've found a new friend, Mitchie," Haley said. "I really like Henry. He's a good kid."

Haley had been worried about Mitchell when they first moved to Hillsdale. She was concerned he wouldn't meet anyone he had anything in common with. And in fact, for the first few months in New Jersey, Mitchell had avoided all social contact with other kids, preferring instead to hang out with his imaginary friend, Marcus.

But now there was Henry. And Haley had been relieved to find out that not only was Henry a real, live boy, but just like Mitchell, he enjoyed robots, found objects, and disassembling light machinery.

"Well, you have my cell phone number in case you decide you want to come home," Haley reminded him.

"Have. A great. Birthday. Haley. And tell Reese. I can finally. Kill. The sea monster. On my own," Mitchell added, referring to the video game he often played with Reese.

Haley took the bus to school and floated through all her classes in a daze. Aside from Cecily and Sasha, no one really seemed to know or care that Haley's birthday fell on Valentine's Day. All the other girls in her grade were too busy accepting bouquets and balloons, or getting their hearts trampled when nothing arrived at their desks. She was forced to watch budding love or total heartbreak happen over and over again, class period after class period.

Clearly, as Haley was discovering, boys took precedence over birthdays in New Jersey.

After school was over for the day, Haley collected her things and hopped a bus to the studio address Sasha had given her. There were no lights on outside when Haley arrived. She opened the unlocked door and stepped inside an empty hallway.

"Sasha?" she called out. Her voice bounced off the walls.

Haley looked into the dark practice spaces one by one. No one else was there, presumably because of the holiday. There wasn't even a clerk or a technician on-site.

A fluorescent light flickered and dimmed above her head. Haley suddenly questioned the laid-back nature of her plans. *Maybe Johnny and Drew surprised the girls with some romantic outing?* Haley considered. There were plenty of things two couples could have spontaneously decided to do on the day of love. *Oh, but then where would Reese be? I guess Coco could have finally gotten her clutches into him.*

Haley adjusted the platinum heirloom locket clasped around her neck, taking comfort in the fact that at least Gam and Mitchell had remembered her birthday. Just as she was about to turn around and walk toward the Exit sign, Haley heard a crash. It sounded like a metal chair falling over, followed by muffled giggles. Haley froze. After a few seconds, she flung open the last practice-room door.

"Surprise!" Sasha, Johnny, Cecily, Drew, Toby, Josh and Reese yelled as they flipped on the lights and popped out from behind metal chairs, instruments, amplifiers and music stands. "Happy Birthday, Haley!"

"Finally!" Haley exclaimed. "I was secretly cursing you guys because I thought you'd dragged me out here for nothing."

Sasha and Cecily had decorated the tiny room with black and white streamers and balloons taped up around the carpeted and soundproofed walls. Cecily, in a hunter green dress over jeans, lit the candles as Sasha, wearing ankle boots and skinny black pants, presented Haley with a tray of pale pink cupcakes. "My mom made them," Sasha said. "It's real French buttercream icing."

"Really?" Haley asked, filled with anticipation.

"Yeah," said Sasha. "Who knew she was such a good cook. Haley, you'll have to come over for dinner one night."

Johnny then led them in a funny round of "Happy Birthday."

"Gosh, thanks, everybody," Haley said humbly, before blowing out her candles.

"Happy sixteenth Valentine's Day, Red," Reese said, taking Haley in his arms. "How could you think even for a second I'd forget?"

"Oh, because everyone else on the planet did,

except for my grandmother and Mitchell," Haley said. "Who, by the way, can now beat the sea monster on his own."

"No way," Reese said. "He's really coming along."

"I know," Haley said, smiling.

"Have a seat," Sasha said. "We have another surprise for you."

Reese sat down on a metal folding chair with Haley on his lap as the band members took their places and picked up instruments.

"The Ivory Lady," Johnny said, presenting Sasha with the old vintage guitar she and Reese had banged around on as kids.

Sasha put the guitar strap over her shoulder and pushed up the sleeves of her gray sweater. Taking a small step toward the microphone, Sasha said softly, "This is a Smiths song called 'There Is a Light That Never Goes Out.'"

Toby led in on the snare drum, followed by the lead guitar, and then Sasha began to sing in smooth, alto tones.

Haley could not believe how good Sasha was. "They're incredible," she whispered to Cecily.

Johnny and Sasha strummed as if they'd been playing together for years. "Because I want to see people," Sasha sang, and Johnny answered, "And I want to see life."

"Yeah!" Cecily yelled and whistled, echoing the sentiments of the three other audience members.

After the Hedon had played through their short set, Haley, Reese, Cecily and Drew congratulated them.

"Guys, I mean it," Haley said passionately. "You are just . . . that was . . . I mean . . . wow."

"Thanks," Sasha said, oblivious to the effect she'd had on her audience.

Haley felt her cell phone vibrate. She looked and saw a text from Mitchell. "R U having a good birthday?" he asked. "Yep," Haley replied. "How is it at Henry's? Do you want me to come pick you up?" She waited patiently for Mitchell's response. "Nope," he wrote. "It's fun here. C U tomorrow." Haley smiled, proud of Mitchell for finally branching out on his own. "Well, just let me know if you need anything," she wrote. "I'll have my cell phone with me all night, and I can be there in five minutes if you need me. xo."

"Mmmm-mmmm, these are tasty cakes," Johnny said, devouring a cupcake. "I may have to steal the rest," he added, winking at Haley.

"Ooh, that reminds me," Cecily said, "I saw the craziest thing on my way over here. Whitney Klein was in the girls' locker room with a pair of pliers, taking one of those plastic metal-detector things off her dress."

"You're kidding! Whitney knows how to use pliers?" Sasha joked.

"Seriously," Cecily said. "You don't think . . ."

"That she's the Bergen County shoplifter the cops are looking for?" Drew asked. "I wouldn't be surprised. I heard her dad recently cut off all her credit cards. Including EUO, Emergency Uses Only."

Interesting, Haley thought, taking another bite of her cupcake.

"Speaking of crazy people," Johnny said with a chuckle. "Did you guys see that kid Shaun's motocross performance art today in the parking lot? He took a dirt bike and launched himself through a flaming heart. All for Irene Chen. It was radical."

"Try insane," said Toby. "I heard that guy got burned pretty badly. He's in the hospital."

"Is he okay?" Haley inquired.

"I don't know, man," Johnny said. "But that was some stunt."

"Well, Haley," Reese said, turning to face her. "I know it's not quite as dramatic as a dirt bike launching through a heart on fire, but I wanted to give you this." He handed her a small wrapped package. "It's just my little way of saying happy Valentine's/ Birthday Day."

Haley unwrapped the box and found a pair of earrings inside. They were clusters of green peridot gems on a set of gold backings. And they were the most beautiful things Haley had ever seen.

● ● ●

Looks as though Haley's finally in with the cool kids. But is this setup too perfect to last?

Sasha Lewis may be just the magic ingredient the Hedon was searching for, but will Sasha be enough to

help them finally achieve their goal of playing a major club in New York City and landing a record deal? Or will the golden couple Johnny and Sasha crack under the pressure?

Ever since Sasha's mom returned from Paris, her life has gotten back on track. If you think Haley should take a closer look at Sasha's new home life, go to page 183.

Think Whitney Klein might be getting into trouble with her compulsive tendencies? Have Haley dig deeper into the shoplifting problem in Bergen County on page 197.

If you believe Haley should be most concerned about Shaun's health and state of mind after that crazy stunt with the flaming heart in the parking lot, visit him in the hospital on page 206.

No matter how you slice the cupcake, that was a great birthday. Now Haley just has to figure out how to turn it into a great year.

What good is popularity
unless you can exploit it?

Ever since Haley Miller had joined social forces with
Sasha Lewis and Cecily Watson, she'd become a part
of the ruling class at Hillsdale High. No one could
touch them. And as long as they were strutting down
hallways together, no one could look away.

Haley was basking in all the attention. On
February fourteenth, Valentine's Day, which just so
happened to be Haley's sweet sixteenth birthday, she
made herself stand out even more by dressing in a
black leather miniskirt, tall boots and a tight, low-
cut red sweater.

Haley's neckline showed off the pretty antique locket Gam Polly had left for her before she had hopped a train home to Pennsylvania. While Gam had said she would've loved to stay for Haley's birthday, she and Haley both knew that Joan and Perry would continue being total workaholics as long as there was someone else around to hold the family together.

Haley wasn't letting it get to her that Gam was now gone. Especially since her smokin' outfit was totally having the desired effect. By the end of the day, nearly everyone at school was talking about "Cupid baby" Haley Miller and just how cute she looked.

Give it up, Annie, Haley thought arrogantly as she read yet another text message from the clingy member of the nerd herd. *I am* not *coming over to your house for cake and ice cream. From now on, you get the digital guillotine: cut off.* Haley callously erased the text without bothering to read the whole thing, much less respond.

As she marched toward her locker to collect her things after the final bell, Haley was still on cloud nine. Her mood only improved when she found dozens of pink and red Valentine's Day and birthday cards crammed into her skinny storage space. *I'll deal with the fan mail later,* she thought, stacking the cards neatly on top of her books.

"Happy birthday, Haley!" a handsome junior football stud yelled from down the hall. "Come see me when you *really* want to celebrate."

The invitation was sort of appealing to Haley. While she had tentatively already made plans to go to the Hedon's band practice after school with Reese, Sasha, Johnny, Cecily and Drew, she began to think about other ways to commemorate her sweet sixteenth.

Her parents couldn't be relied upon to pull through with a last-minute party—they were so busy with their own work schedules, Haley was pretty certain they had forgotten her birthday entirely. But with Gam gone, and her parents at their respective offices until at least midnight, Haley suddenly realized that the house would likely be empty for the next eight or nine hours.

Haley opened her cell phone and typed out a text message to just about everyone she knew, leaving off Sasha, Cecily and the boys, whose idea of celebrating, after all, seemed to be listening to a bunch of amateurs strum their guitars all night. *I deserve to have a sweet sixteen just like everyone else,* Haley told herself just before hitting Send. *And even if I do get caught, I bet Mom and Dad will feel so guilty about forgetting my birthday, they won't even mind.*

When Perry Miller pulled into the driveway that evening at ten o'clock, with a guilty look on his face and an ice cream cake melting on the passenger seat, there were six hooligans on the front lawn toilet-papering a pair of spruce trees, and three couples either making out or smoking cigarettes on the porch. Through the bay window, Perry could see girls dancing wildly on the Millers' heirloom coffee table, and two skater boys looking up their skirts.

As he entered the hip-hop club formerly known as his home, Perry didn't look shocked by what he encountered inside. He looked horrified.

He finally located Haley in the kitchen, where she was doing gelatin shots with the studly junior football player. "Where's Mitchell," Perry demanded in a tone Haley had never heard from him before.

"Relax," Haley said angrily. "I sent him to his friend Henry's."

"Have you lost your mind?" Perry asked as a group of boys continued chugging their beer at the Millers' kitchen table. "You're supposed to watch him after school! And instead, you send him to a complete stranger's house?"

"It's my birthday," Haley countered. "Or don't I get a day off from raising your kid for that?"

Perry picked up the phone and dialed the police station.

"Yo, po po's coming," one of the beer guzzlers said, and within seconds, the warning had ricocheted through the party. As the crowd dispersed, Perry next turned to Haley with the receiver still in his hand. In a somewhat embarrassed tone, he asked, "What's Henry's last name?"

"Awesome," Haley said. "Mitchell finally makes a friend here, and you've got no idea who he is. Even

Gam met his parents." Haley grabbed two gelatin shots and sat down at the now-empty kitchen table while Perry dialed Joan's cell phone number.

"Can I speak to my wife," Perry asked through gritted teeth. Haley listened as Perry gave her mother a rundown of the night's events. Not surprisingly, Joan hadn't the faintest clue who Henry was either. She did tell Perry, however, that she had asked Annie to get in touch with Haley several times throughout the day, to let her know that Mitchell was overdue for a visit to his therapist.

Guess those texts from Annie were important after all, Haley realized. *I hope Mitchell's all right.*

Just then, the phone rang. It was Henry's mother, calling to say that Mitchell needed to be picked up immediately. He'd had a meltdown and had now stopped talking entirely.

Perry took down the address, hopped back into the car and raced to go get him, leaving Haley to clean up the party mess all on her own.

Oddly enough, the severe punishment Haley received from Perry later that night wasn't what hurt her the most. It was the feeling that she had somehow let Mitchell down. It took him weeks to be able to leave the house on his own again, and months before he was ready to spend the night at Henry's.

What's more, Haley later found out that Sasha and Cecily had been planning a surprise birthday party for her that night at the Hedon's studio. Not only had she left them in the dark, literally, by not calling to say she wasn't coming, but Haley hadn't invited her two best friends and sort-of boyfriend to the house party she'd thrown for her own sweet sixteen.

That, needless to say, marked the end of her relationship with Reese, and the end of her friendship with Sasha and Cecily, and it began Haley's life as an antisocial teenager trapped in a small bedroom on restriction with no friends.

● ● ●

Hang your head and go back to page I.

Breaking hearts is not a crime punishable by law, but maybe it should be.

"*¡Feliz cumpleaños, Mariposa!*" Ms. Frick wrote on the chalkboard in a flowery pink script. She took one step to her right and began drawing a big heart.

Haley looked around awkwardly. It pained her to wait for someone to translate the teacher's embarrassing announcement that today was her birthday. Though that someone was certainly not going to be either of Hillsdale High's recently deposed teen queens, Coco De Clerq and Whitney Klein.

"I thought you maxed out *el credito*?" Coco asked

Whitney as she glared suspiciously at the plum-colored dress Whitney had on. Both girls seemed completely oblivious to the lesson going on in front of them.

"*Mi el credito* was not maxed out-o," Whitney said defensively. "Anyways. In more important news, my dad flaked on another court date. We think he's in the Bahamas with Trish. If he doesn't show one more time, the judge is going to rule in my mother's favor. And then she'll get everything, including the house."

"Students?" Ms. Frick asked, still waiting for a translating volunteer.

"Well, there's a shocker," Coco said snidely as Annie Armstrong's arm shot up into the air.

Ms. Frick turned around, happy to finally have at least one student eager to participate. Even if that one student was the brownnoser Annie Armstrong.

"*Sí.*" The teacher called on Annie.

"Happy birthday, Haley!" Annie announced exuberantly. "And . . . Happy Valentine's Day!"

Whitney did a double take at the chalkboard, finally realizing what it said. "Haley's B-day is on V-day?"

"*Cocita, silencio,*" Ms. Frick reprimanded, with her back still turned away from her students. She was listing assignments on the board.

"*Excusez-moi?*" Coco said in French, offended she'd been falsely accused of talking out of turn. At least that time.

"Do you know what you're getting for your birthday?" Annie whispered to Haley. Coco and Whitney looked mildly interested. Haley shook her head. She was too embarrassed to admit that both of her work-obsessed parents had seemingly forgotten her birthday altogether.

"Oh, I did get this," Haley said, lifting up the antique locket that was hanging around her neck.

"That's beautiful," Annie cooed.

"Gorg," Coco agreed. "Heirloom jewelry is so hot right now."

"¡Cocita!" Ms. Frick snapped again. Coco looked cross.

"You should stop by the Armstrong and White offices sometime," Annie suggested to Haley. "Your mom's *always* there."

Tell me about it, Haley thought. *I'm getting a little fed up with it.*

Ms. Frick turned back around. "Now, students, we are going to discuss what Valentine's Day means for each of us." Sebastian Bodega casually raised his hand.

"*Sí, Sebastian.*" Ms. Frick called on the dark and swarthy Spanish exchange student, whose jet black hair had been neatly trimmed for his meetings with college swimming scouts.

Wow, he looks really cute these days, Haley observed, admiring Sebastian's clean-cut new look.

Ms. Frick turned to face the board once again,

intending to transcribe Sebastian's answer. But instead of addressing Ms. Frick at the front of the room, Sebastian turned around in his chair to look at Haley. In Spanish he professed, "May this year be sweeter than any year you've tasted in life. Smell the roses, *mi Valentín*. You are so very beautiful. I am seeing stars."

Haley blushed bright red. *"Gracias,"* she whispered.

"Come to Spain with me for spring break," he whispered back. "I will not rest until you say yes."

"¡Qué bonito, Sebbie!" Ms. Frick said, spinning around on her heel and clasping her hands together passionately. "Sebastian, I had no idea you felt that way, though the classroom is hardly the appropriate place to declare such sentiments." Her voice fell an octave when she added, "See me after class."

Haley suddenly realized Ms. Frick assumed Sebastian had been talking to *her*. *Ew,* she thought, grossed out by her teacher's obvious attraction to the hot Spanish import.

"What was all that gobbledygook Sebastian was saying to Haley?" Whitney asked Coco.

"It's *Día de Valentín*," Coco stated. "He probably told her he's in love with her and wants to make little Spanish babies in the backseat of his European compact."

Just then, there was a loud knock at the door. Through the glass, Haley could see a deliveryman with an enormous bouquet of long-stemmed red roses. Haley took out her video camera and set it on top of her desk discreetly. As the deliveryman entered, she pressed Record.

"*¿Hola?*" Ms. Frick said as she sashayed over to the door. "Are these for me?" she asked, taking the flowers and hugging them to her breast dramatically as she eyed Sebastian.

"Nope," said the deliveryman. "They're for . . ." He paused and scanned his clipboard.

Whitney squirmed impatiently. "Who do you think they're for?" she asked Coco.

"Well, obviously one of us," Coco replied. "Who else in this geek squad would be getting roses on Valentine's Day?"

Haley glanced around the room, wondering exactly the same thing. Annie was smiling brightly at Dave, but he shrugged with an apologetic look on his face, which made it clear he hadn't sent them. The shrimpy Hannah Moss, who didn't look much older than twelve, was busy taking apart a cell phone on her desk. *There's no way she's getting any roses this year,* Haley decided. *Not until she hits a growth spurt.*

"Miss De Clerq?" the deliveryman said, looking up. Ms. Frick frowned, and clutched the roses possessively.

"*¿Si?*" Coco said, acting surprised.

"I've been instructed to tell you . . ." He looked

down at the attached card and read, "'Coco, you are too hot for words. Love, your secret admirer.'"

"Well, I wonder who that could be?" Coco asked innocently, looking around the room to make sure *everyone* had heard the message.

"Well, that's easy enough to find out," Annie said, playing the sleuth as she got up from her desk. "There's an invoice attached. Let's just read the name on the credit card slip."

"No!" Coco shouted, lunging out of her chair. "I mean, why would you want to do that? It spoils the mystery."

Annie continued unabated. "The cardholder's name is—"

"Really, Annie," Coco interrupted.

"Coco De Clerq?" the deliveryman announced.

Haley gasped.

"No it's not," Coco insisted. "I did not send those flowers to myself! I have a secret admirer! I do! I do!" Coco grabbed the vase from Ms. Frick and threw the roses to the floor before storming out of the class.

"Huh." Whitney laughed nervously. "Self-love is the new true love," she added, in Coco's defense.

"Hear that?" a kid with bottle-thick glasses and scaly skin called out from the back of the room. "Coco De Clerq is into self-love."

The class erupted in laughter.

Guess Coco's plan to regain her popularity after that awful scene on New Year's isn't quite working,

Haley thought, recalling Coco's spectacular downfall a few weeks back. Coco had gotten plastered, publicly declared her unrequited love for Reese Highland, accused Spencer Eton and her sister, Ali, of getting it on when they weren't and then, to top it all off, thrown up in Richie's hot tub. *It's going to take a lot more than a vase of flowers to get people to respect and admire her again,* Haley thought, turning off her video camera. *Not even a* vat *of roses could save Coco's reputation at this point.*

● ● ●

What a birthday gift that was. Haley just caught Coco De Clerq sending herself roses on video. Looks as if Haley has captured yet another humiliating moment to add to Coco's stock of shame. Fortunately, no one knew Haley was filming. Otherwise, they'd all want to see the instant replay.

If you think it's weird that Whitney's always wearing new clothes when supposedly her credit has been cut off, go INVESTIGATE WHITNEY on page 197.

If you're less concerned with Whitney's clothing allowance and more concerned with Mr. Klein skipping out on his divorce court dates, see what Whitney's home life is currently like on page 190.

Finally, was Sebastian's love confession for real? Or was that just his melodramatic way of getting extra credit with Ms. Frick by showing off his romance language skills? And when will Haley get her next chance to find out? Right now, the only possibility for a glimpse at Sebastian is to head to Armstrong & White with Annie and Dave on page 201.

Have Haley investigate the queen of diamonds or seek out the king of hearts. But make sure you know when to hold, fold or run.

HOME-BAKED BIRTHDAY

All it takes to make a birthday party is two people, a candle and a cupcake.

Haley woke up on Valentine's Day, which also happened to be her sixteenth birthday, still wondering what her friends had planned for her. Ever since Sebastian had invited her to Spain for spring break, he had been somewhat MIA around campus. Between the college recruiting trips and his private English lessons with Ms. Lipsky, he didn't seem to have any time left for Haley. And he certainly wasn't showering her with his usual amount of affection.

Annie and Dave, meanwhile, were preoccupied

with the yearbook committee. And at home, things were hardly any better.

Haley's parents were working constantly and were hardly ever around. And after staying on for a few weeks past Christmas to look after the kids, Gam Polly was now back at home in Pennsylvania. She said she would have loved to stay for Haley's birthday, but ultimately, she felt Perry and Joan would never face their problems as long as someone else was around to hold the family together. So, Gam had packed her bags, leaving Haley and Mitchell to fend for themselves with a few frozen lasagnas and a stack of takeout menus.

Haley wondered if her parents even realized that it was Valentine's Day, much less her birthday. At this point, she would have been happy if Perry and Joan had decided to take off for a romantic weekend alone. Anything, just so long as they were together and happy and not sequestered in their respective offices.

Once Haley had fully woken up, she made her way downstairs in her pajamas. "Hello? Anyone home?" There was no breakfast waiting on the table, and Haley found that the refrigerator had been drained of both orange juice and milk. "Great," Haley muttered. "I get to scrape together breakfast on my birthday."

"Good. Morning," Mitchell said, handing her a poorly wrapped package. He had already dressed himself for school, in a brown plaid shirt and bright green pants. Haley noticed he was wearing two different shoes.

"Hey, buddy," she said. "What's this?" She opened the present and found it was an old flashlight with a cardboard snowflake attached to the end. She flicked it on and it cast a pattern of light on the ceiling. "Cool," she said.

"Henry. Helped. Me make it," Mitchell said.

Haley was thrilled that Mitchell had finally made a real friend in Hillsdale. Especially since he'd spent the first few months after the move hanging out only with his imaginary pal, Marcus.

"Henry's mom taking you to school again today?" she asked.

"Affirmative," said Mitchell. "And I am. Going to his house. After school."

"Well, just let me know if you need to be picked up," said Haley. "I've always got my cell phone with me. Honest, if you ever need anything, just call or text me."

Mitchell nodded. "I should. Text you now. Hungry," he said, holding his stomach.

"Well then, how about some pancakes?" Haley asked, locating some just-add-water mix in the pantry.

"Affirmative."

After their yummy pancake birthday breakfast, Haley put Mitchell into the car with Henry's mom and then caught the bus to school herself. She wasn't expecting any miracles, but still, her day seemed to be getting only worse after she arrived. There were no notes, or balloons, or single red roses tucked into her locker. *It's like some sort of cosmic double whammy,* Haley decided. *Not only did practically everyone I know—including my parents!—forget my sixteenth birthday, but no one even sent me a Valentine.*

Finally, just before her third class of the day, Haley got a text message from Annie. *Thank goodness for loyal, dependable Annie Armstrong,* Haley thought, remembering Annie's long-standing invitation to do cake and ice cream at her house after school. But the text was just to explain that Annie would be in meetings with the typesetter all day for yearbook. She asked if Haley wouldn't mind meeting her later to help her choose fonts for a few layouts. *Amazing,* Haley thought, heading off to the cafeteria to pout and each lunch alone.

By the time three o'clock rolled around, Haley was feeling pretty low. All day, her torment had been exacerbated by the giant bouquets of flowers, big boxes of chocolates and thick love letters that had arrived on other girls' desks, in honor of Valentine's Day.

This will go down as the absolute worst birthday in history, Haley thought. *Plus, I'm sixteen now and I don't even get to drive because of New Jersey's stupid traffic laws!* As the final bell of the day rang, Haley thought, *At least it's almost over.* She collected her books from her locker and put them in her backpack, where she found a box from Gam. Inside was an old, intricate locket.

> *Dear Haley,*
> *I so wish I could have stayed to celebrate your birthday with you. Sixteen is such a special year.*
> *My mother gave me this locket on my sixteenth birthday, and from the moment I put it on, I was a little more sure of myself, a little more aware of who I wanted to be in the world.*
> *You have so many happy experiences to look forward to this year. Take care of Mitchell and your parents for me.*
> *Love always,*
> *Gam*

Haley bit her lip and put the locket on. It was the first gift from her grandmother in recent memory that didn't involve a stocking stitch.

Guess she's finally starting to see me as a grown-up, Haley thought, wandering into the parking lot in search of the Armstrongs' minivan.

Haley wasn't exactly looking forward to doing menial yearbook work with Annie on her birthday, but then, it's not as if she had anything better to do.

"Hi, Haley," Annie's dad, Doug, said as Haley climbed into the backseat.

"What do you mean you need a smaller file?" Annie practically yelled into her cell phone, without bothering to acknowledge her father's or Haley's presence. "You asked me for high res and I gave you high res! I don't care if it doesn't. Make it work!" She snapped her phone shut. "I cannot believe how incompetent these people are."

"So, I guess I don't have to ask how your day went," Haley mumbled, knowing Annie wouldn't even think to ask about hers.

"Clearly, you and I still have a lot of work to do," Annie said. "I hope you planned on pulling an all-nighter."

Haley shrugged and gave in to the inevitable. If her birthday was going to suck, it might as well be a spectacular failure. "Mitchell's at Henry's for the night, so I guess I could stay over."

What she wasn't prepared for, however, was the surprise she received when she walked into the Armstrongs' kitchen.

There, sitting around the table behind a home-baked birthday cake, were Dave, Sebastian, Hannah Moss and Dale Smithwick, a skinny kid with dark skin from some of Haley's classes. Haley knew Annie had been trying to fix up Dale with Hannah, presumably as a precaution to keep Hannah away from Dave. Aside from Sebastian and maybe Dave, this wasn't exactly the crowd Haley had envisioned surrounding her at her sixteenth birthday. But then, she wasn't really in a position to complain.

"Happy birthday, Haley!" Dave and Hannah called out.

"Um, wow, I wasn't expecting . . . *this,*" Haley said, unsure of what to do next.

"We would've thrown you a real party except . . . well, your birthday's on Valentine's Day," Annie said. "Do you know how hard it is to find a venue that's free, much less anyone without a date who can come?"

"Valentine's Day is awesome," Dave said, sighing and staring at his lady love, Annie.

"For some people," Dale said. "Did you hear about what happened to that kid Shaun? He was trying to impress Irene Chen, and he rode his motorbike through a flaming heart in the parking lot."

"That was inspired," Annie said, eyeing Dave.

"He's in the hospital," Dale added.

"That was stupid." Annie corrected herself.

"Is he okay?" Haley asked.

"Dunno yet," said Dale.

"Haley," Sebastian said, rising from the table, "I had planned for you a beautiful birthday and Valentine's Day dinner tonight. We shall eat, and dance, and you can finally give me your answer about Spain and spring break."

Haley blushed.

"What is it? Are you afraid? Annie and Dave will be coming," Sebastian continued.

"Yeah, I'm going to need such a vacation after yearbook," Annie said dramatically.

"And my parents will be there to chaperone," Sebastian added.

"Speaking of parents, where are Haley's?" Dale whispered to Hannah, just loud enough for Haley to hear. Hannah shook her head tersely and frowned at him, signaling that this was not an appropriate topic for discussion.

But even Haley couldn't let it go. *Where are my parents?* she wondered as she sampled the birthday cake and opened her presents from her friends. *How could they have forgotten? Why are they avoiding each other? And what exactly is going on between them?*

Those questions were still bothering her later that night, over a romantic dinner with Sebastian. The problem was, Haley wasn't really sure if she wanted the answers yet. All she knew was that she'd have to confront Joan and Perry sooner or later, especially if she decided to go to Spain. And at this point, getting out of Hillsdale for a while seemed like the best available option.

● ● ●

The situation with Haley's parents can't get any worse. Or can it?

If you think it's time Haley dealt with her mom and dad, then send her to find out WHAT'S GOING ON at the Armstrong & White offices on page 201, where she can also ask about that trip to Spain.

If you want Haley to avoid her parents altogether,

and wait for them to come and apologize to her, then have her VISIT SHAUN in the hospital on page 206.

Whether she's prepping for a Spain trip, or checking on a boy with bad burns and a sprain, Haley's mind is likely to keep drifting back to her mom and dad. But is it her job to remind them of their duties as parents? Or will they snap out of it and step up on their own?

**An empty house might
seem like every kid's
dream, but it can be a
nightmare not having
parents around.**

Haley woke up on her sweet sixteenth birthday,
which also happened to be Valentine's Day, still wondering what her parents had planned for her.

Joan and Perry were clearly going through an off
time, and more and more, they seemed to be focusing
on their work instead of dealing with each other and
their kids. But even so, Haley assumed they would
get it together long enough to help her celebrate.
Boy, was she ever wrong.

After putting on her baby blue bathrobe, Haley

opened her bedroom door to find a seemingly empty house. That is, except for Freckles, who clearly needed to go out.

Not even Gam Polly was there to greet Haley, since she had returned home to Pennsylvania a few days prior. Gam had said she would have loved to stay for Haley's birthday, but she figured Joan and Perry would keep avoiding each other as long as there was someone else in the house to keep the family together. And it was best if they started facing their problems, and each other.

That left Haley and Mitchell to fend for themselves with a few frozen lasagnas in the fridge and a stack of takeout menus. Not exactly an ideal way to celebrate.

Haley heard a noise coming from Mitchell's room. "Hey, buddy, you still here?" she asked, knocking on his door.

"Mrs. Yellen. Is. Picking me up. At half past eight," Mitchell said, handing Haley two packages. One was an old flashlight with a cardboard snowflake attached—clearly a Mitchell project. Haley flicked it on and they watched as a pattern of light skipped around the room, looking not unlike snow. Mitchell had scrawled the words *Happy Valirthday* across the side.

Haley smiled. "Thanks, buddy. You didn't have to do that."

"Someone had. To. Remember. Your birthday."

The second item was a small box bearing Haley's name in her grandmother's handwriting. Inside were a letter and an intricate heirloom locket.

> *Dear Haley,*
> *I so wish I could have stayed to celebrate your birthday with you. Sixteen is such a special year.*
> *My mother gave me this locket on my sixteenth birthday, and from the moment I put it on, I was a little more sure of myself, a little more aware of who I wanted to be in the world.*
> *You have so many happy experiences to look forward to this year, Haley. And I know that you'll continue to take care of Mitchell and your parents for me.*
> *Love always,*
> *Gam*

Haley wiped a tear off her cheek.

"Haley," Mitchell asked, crawling into her lap. "Are we. Orphans."

Haley laughed. "No, buddy. Mom and Dad will come around eventually. In the meantime, what do you say to a pancake breakfast? And then later, I can meet you here after school and we can go out for pizza to celebrate, just you and me. How's that sound?"

Mitchell nodded and Haley packed his backpack so that after breakfast, they could meet Mrs. Yellen outside. Mrs. Yellen was the mother of Henry Yellen, Mitchell's first new friend in Hillsdale. Haley was relieved Mitchell had finally found someone his own age to play with. Especially since, for the first few months after the Millers had moved east, Mitchell had insisted on hanging out only with his imaginary friend, Marcus.

Later that morning, after Haley had made pancakes for her and Mitchell and cleaned up the kitchen, she caught the bus to school. Unfortunately, there were no birthday notes, or balloons, or Valentines stuck to her locker. Nor did any arrive throughout the day. Not even a birthday e-mail from her old friend in California, Gretchen Waller.

Her torment was exacerbated when, period after period, she had to watch as giant bouquets of red roses, big boxes of chocolates and thick love letters kept arriving on other girls' desks.

It's like some sort of cosmic double whammy, Haley decided as the last bell of the day rang. *Not only did my parents forget my sixteenth birthday, but no one even sent me a Valentine.*

Just then, Haley got a text message from, of all people, Hannah Moss. *So someone finally figured it out,* Haley thought, opening up her phone and retrieving the text. But it was a mass message about Shaun. He'd just ridden his motorbike through a flaming heart in the parking lot to impress Irene Chen, and now he was in the hospital.

Guess someone is having a worse day than I am, Haley thought, hoping that Shaun was all right.

Haley then got a text from Annie. She assumed it would be a long apology followed by a last-minute birthday invite, but instead, all it said was: "Stuck in yearbook meetings all day. You thought any more about Sebastian's invitation to go to Spain for spring break? Dave and I are totally in, but it won't be the same without you . . . AA."

Then, just before Haley boarded the bus to take her home, Cecily Watson tracked her down. Haley thought maybe *she* was coming over to wish her a happy birthday, but instead, Cecily just wanted to know if Haley had noticed anything unusual about Whitney Klein's behavior lately. Cecily was convinced that Whitney was Bergen County's now-infamous shoplifter, and she said she thought someone ought to help Whitney before she got caught. The police, Cecily had heard, were setting up a sting operation.

Okay, Haley thought, *so two people are having worse days than I am. Somehow, that doesn't make me feel better.*

Haley was feeling pretty low when she returned, once again, to an empty house. *This will go down as the absolute worst birthday in history,* she thought, plopping down on the sofa without even bothering to turn on any lights. *Plus, I'm sixteen now and I don't even get to drive because of these stupid New Jersey traffic laws!*

Then she remembered Mitchell. And her grandmother's note. Haley knew in an instant that she couldn't afford to mope around anymore. Not since she was now basically taking care of Mitchell all on her own. At least until her parents woke up from their work-induced haze.

She changed her clothes, brushed her hair, put on some new lip gloss and waited downstairs in the Millers' kitchen for Mitchell to come home. *Pizza will make me feel better,* she thought. *Pizza can solve anything.*

Plus, there were, Haley had to admit, other things to look forward to. Like, for instance, the possibility of going to Spain for spring break with Sebastian Bodega, Annie Armstrong and Dave Metzger. A trip like that would make up for a dozen missed birthdays. Provided she could actually find her parents and get their permission to go.

● ● ●

Okay, so that was pretty much a total disaster. Haley's parents, her friends, her crushes—basically everyone in her life except for Mitchell and her grandmother—forgot all about her big milestone birthday.

But then, leave it to Haley Miller to look on the bright side.

Now, she's off to pizza with Mitchell. But what's next? To have Haley confront her parents and find out WHAT'S GOING ON, send her to the offices of Armstrong & White on page 201. To VISIT SHAUN in the hospital, turn to page 206. Or have Haley INVESTI-GATE WHITNEY on page 197.

Sure, you can break hearts, but did you know you can also set them on fire?

It was Valentine's Day, and more importantly, Haley's sixteenth birthday, and she was determined not to let the fact that her parents had clearly forgotten both holidays spoil her day.

Besides, at least two family members had remembered. Mitchell had given Haley a pair of presents that morning. The first was an old flashlight with a cardboard snowflake attached. When Haley turned it on, it cast a pattern of light on the ceiling that looked not unlike snow. Mitchell had even scrawled the words *Happy Valirthday* on the side in his messy handwriting.

The second gift was a small box from her grandmother. Inside were a letter and an intricate old platinum locket.

> *Dear Haley,*
>
> *I so wish I could have stayed to celebrate your birthday with you. Sixteen is such a special year.*
>
> *My mother gave me this locket on my sixteenth birthday, and from the moment I put it on, I was a little more sure of myself, a little more aware of who I wanted to be in the world.*
>
> *You have so many happy experiences to look forward to this year. And I know that you'll continue to take care of Mitchell and your parents for me.*
> *Love always,*
> *Gam*

It was the first gift from Gam in recent memory that didn't involve a stocking stitch.

Haley put the locket on and headed off to school. When she arrived, Devon was waiting for her with balloons, a box of chocolates, roses and a noisemaker.

"I wasn't sure what to do for a birthday that falls on Valentine's Day, so I just went all out," he said, giving Haley a kiss on the cheek. Haley knew he'd probably spent a week's paycheck from the vintage shop where he worked, which made the gifts all the more special.

Devon and Irene had clearly reminded everyone they knew that it was Haley's birthday, so all day, various kids from the Floods, some of whom Haley had never even met before, kept coming up to her to wish her a happy sweet sixteenth.

All in all, it was a great day. Until . . .

Shaun had announced during art class that morning that he planned to present his big project that afternoon. So, at two-thirty, Mr. Von and his students reconvened in the parking lot to await Shaun's "installation."

Haley figured his presentation would have something to do with his recent professional eating obsession. But boy, was she ever wrong.

Before Mr. Von could figure out what was going on, much less stop him, Shaun appeared at the far end of the parking lot in head-to-toe leather, wearing goggles and a cape. He squatted down on a motorized dirtbike that, Haley noticed, was more than a little too small for his frame.

"Irene Chen," Shaun yelled. He was almost giddy with excitement. "I'm a fool for love! And you made me that way. My little Zen flower, my muse, I am in love with you. This is all for you. Troll, light the fuse."

"No," Irene whispered. She took a step forward. "No!" she screamed. "Shaun!"

But it was too late. On the other side of the parking lot, the Troll, who was standing in front of a large ramp with a big curtain obscuring a tall structure, pulled on a cord and the curtain fell, revealing a huge wire heart. As Shaun revved his engine, the Troll struck a match and tossed it into the air. The heart was suddenly engulfed in flames.

Shaun tore through the parking lot on the motorbike, weaving and wobbling and sputtering on his way toward the ramp. Haley could tell he wasn't building up enough speed. In the seconds before Shaun hit the ramp, Haley turned her head, so she didn't see the bike falter. Or Shaun go tumbling headfirst through the flaming heart. She didn't see him land on the concrete behind it. But she did see Irene, who had watched the whole grizzly scene, go weak in the knees. Haley got there just in time to catch her friend as she fainted.

From the groans coming from Shaun's general direction, Haley knew this was not going to be good.

●　●　●

Uh-oh. Haley's birthday was going so well, and then this had to happen. Shaun could have seriously injured himself with that ridiculous stunt. There's no telling how much damage he's done to his body. At best, he'll be scarred for life. And still, he might not end up with Irene.

To VISIT SHAUN in the hospital, turn to page 206.

To PUSH IRENE'S BUTTONS and force her to confront Shaun's undying affection, turn to page 211.

If you think Haley should be mad at Shaun for doing something so dumb to try and win over Irene, and think it's more important for Haley to find out WHAT'S GOING ON with her absentee parents, send her to the offices of Armstrong & White on page 201.

Time heals all wounds. Except when they're inflicted by a mini dirtbike and a fiery heart.

Life can get pretty heady
when your mom is
a shrink.

Sasha's initial reaction when her mother showed back up in Hillsdale after so many years away was one of anger and distrust. But after a few weeks, once Mrs. Lewis had a chance to explain that she had only stayed in France to finish her degree and ensure that she could support her daughter on her own, Sasha had softened and begun to let her mother back into her life.

Now, the mother-daughter duo had settled into a cozy routine in their rented Craftsman bungalow in the Heights. Whatever harm had been done over the past year seemed to melt away with each passing day. Having her mother stateside was acting as a stabilizing force in Sasha's life. Now there was always someone to talk to, about Johnny, the band, anything at all.

On weekends, Sasha and her mom would venture into New York together, to shop or have lunch at one of the big department stores. They visited galleries downtown and museums uptown, went to the ballet and ate dinner in the best French restaurants. According to Pascale, Sasha needed to learn what a real happy meal consisted of: steak au poivre, frisée salad and frites.

The New York jaunts were to make up for the fact that they were living in the culturally challenged New Jersey suburbs, Pascale explained. During the week, when they were stuck at home, there was always a delicious French provincial meal on the table, along with lessons of what life was like in Paris.

"Mmmm," Cecily moaned, taking another bite of Mrs. Lewis's homemade crepes slathered with chocolate sauce and sautéed bananas.

"Delicious," Haley agreed. Sasha had invited both girls over to sample her mother's cooking on Tuesday night.

"Aren't they even better than the savory ones with ham and Brie?" Sasha said, devouring another crepe. Dressed in a gray wool military jacket her mother had bought for her in the city, and a white tank top and jeans, Sasha looked like her old stunning self. "Mama, I just loooove your cooking," she cooed.

Mrs. Lewis was standing by the stove in a belted brown turtleneck swing dress and suede boots, looking not nearly old enough to have a daughter in high school. "It is because you have been living on such junk all this time, Sashette," Mrs. Lewis said, using her adorable nickname for her daughter. "You are just for the first time beginning to *taste*."

Cecily sighed. "Sasha, your mom is the most stylish woman on the planet."

"I know," Haley added. What she was thinking was, *My mom couldn't be less stylish if she tried. And now, thanks to this case, she's lucky to get out of the house with matching shoes and socks.*

It was a mystery to Haley how some women were in possession of truly great style like Mrs. Lewis, while others simply used clothes to keep warm and cover up. With Pascale, no matter what she did, whether it was dusting a lampshade or entertaining a group of guests for dinner, it was done with such skill that it seemed almost like art.

Haley marveled at her efficiency. In the short time since Mrs. Lewis had returned from France, she had decorated the new bungalow like a French country cottage, rescued Sasha from paternal abandonment, set up her own psychiatry practice in a back office of the house and welcomed several regular clients, including Haley's younger brother, Mitchell.

"You know, Haley," Pascale said warmly, flipping a fresh batch of strawberry crepes onto the oven-warmed plate and setting them in front of the girls. "Your brother is highly intelligent."

"Really?" Haley said. "Weird" was a comment she expected to hear about Mitchell, or "deeply odd" or "disturbed." But not "highly intelligent." That was a surprise.

"Really. He's exceptional," Pascale said. "Today he solved a college-level math problem."

"Cool," Haley said, taking a bite of her crepe.

"I've tried to explain this to your parents, but they seem so busy. Mitchell should be in a special school, where there are teachers who know how to stimulate him."

Haley nodded and took another bite of the steaming hot crepe. She wasn't quite sure what she was supposed to do with this information. Pass it on to the parents she rarely saw anymore, because they were both constantly working and only came home to shower and sleep? Enroll Mitchell in a new school herself?

"So you're saying there's definitely nothing . . . wrong with him?" Haley asked tentatively.

"Not in the slightest," said Pascale. "He is just, like so many geniuses and artists in this world, simply misunderstood."

"Speaking of misunderstood," Sasha said, looking at her mom.

"Sashette, please. No more talk of your father."

"But don't you think we should both go and see him? If only to hear what he has to say for himself?"

"When I wrote to you, after I left for Paris to try and make a life for us together, you tore up my letters and never wrote me back. Your father's mistakes are much greater than mine, and already, you are rushing to forgive him. This, I do not understand."

"You *chose* to go. Daddy was powerless over his addictions. It's a disease." Sasha looked down at her shoes. "He sold the condo last weekend."

"Yes, I heard," Pascale said lightly. "Linda Klein was the listing agent. I would have guessed he would have used Ron Latham, since they were old friends. But perhaps Mrs. Klein offered him a better prospect?" Pascale raised an eyebrow. "A shame she and Jerry split. They were such a . . . well-matched couple."

"She's just Daddy's real estate agent, Mama," Sasha assured her mother. "There's nothing going on."

"Not that I care, but I'm not so sure," Pascale said frankly.

"Speaking of the Kleins," Cecily said, casually steering the subject away from loaded talk about Sasha's dad's love life. "Whitney has gotten herself in big trouble."

"What's the Cocobot done now?" Sasha asked.

"She was caught shoplifting. The police have evidence."

"No way," Haley gasped.

"Girls," Pascale said, chiding their gossipy tone. "If Whitney is struggling with some obsessive-compulsive tendencies, she will need help and compassion from her friends, not idle chatter."

Just then, the doorbell rang. It was mainly just a courtesy, since Johnny Lane, Drew Napolitano and Reese Highland let themselves in, still wearing their sweaty gym clothes, having come straight over from basketball practice.

"What's cookin', good lookin'?" Drew said, planting a kiss on Cecily's lips.

Reese planted one on Haley's cheek, then pulled up a chair to the table.

"Hey," Johnny said, kissing the top of Sasha's head as he grabbed a strawberry crepe and shoved it into his mouth.

"Boys," Pascale said, swatting Johnny's hand with a spatula. "There are plenty of crepes to go around. But no one comes to my table unshaven and unshowered. There are two bathrooms at the top of the steps. Reese, you can use the one at the back, next to my office. You'll find everything you need— towels, razors—under the sink."

As the boys filed off to the showers, Pascale stepped up to the stove once again and fired it up to make the next batch of crepes.

● ● ●

It's a sweet life for Sasha now that her mother's back in town. There are clearly some big perks to having a mom with highly evolved taste in clothes and highly evolved taste buds.

But what do you think of the fact that Sasha's dad has a new "Realtor" in Mrs. Linda Klein? No wonder Sasha's testy about even the thought of her father's new relationship. How would you feel if your dad were dating a grown-up version of Whitney Klein?

If you think Haley should help Sasha try to reunite her parents, then find out what happens when you mix oil and water at the local Italian restaurant on page 214.

If you're convinced Haley would rather save Whitney from her compulsive behavior, then GET HELP FOR WHITNEY on page 220.

Finally, if you want Mitchell to be Haley's priority, then send her to confront her workaholic mom on page 233.

It must be rough for Haley to see a family life that's so functional, given her current situation. Now that Sasha's life is back on track, maybe it's time for things to change in the Miller home.

ESTATE SALE

People who work in real estate are almost never real.

Ever since Whitney's mother had started attending Alcoholics Anonymous meetings, she had totally turned her life around. Of course, Linda Klein wasn't *really* an alcoholic, as Haley and just about all Whitney's friends well knew. But with Linda's soon-to-be-*ex*-husband Jerry freezing all her assets, and her only available funds going to divorce attorneys, who had money for therapy?

AA had become a place for Mrs. Klein to sort through her feelings and regain control of her life. She just had to occasionally remember to throw in a

190

sordid tale about being "loaded" or "wasted" and how that had affected her life so that none of the other members would suspect.

In spite of all the lying, AA had been good for Mrs. Klein. The support of her "fellow" alcoholics had helped her muster up the courage to get her real estate license and start a new career.

Actually, it was her first career, and the first real steady job she'd had in her entire adult life.

Real estate was an absolutely perfect fit for Mrs. Klein. All she had to do was look in her Rolodex and merge two of her golden lists: well-heeled friends who were always looking to buy if the property and price were right, and restless owners of the best real estate in all of Bergen County, who could always be tempted by a few extra zeros.

Linda used her connections at the local country club to keep track of anyone who was considering moving into or out of Hillsdale, and at least one day a week, she would stake out a local funeral parlor, scouting for potential "motivated sellers."

For all these reasons and more, Linda Klein was fast becoming a real threat to Ron Latham Properties, the top and oldest real estate agency in Hillsdale. And she was positively determined to overtake him in sales by year's end.

Now, spending a Saturday afternoon with Whitney usually meant helping her mom stage a property, deliver documents or turn over keys. Which is why Whitney and Haley were currently riding around in Linda's old clunker, checking out For Sale signs while on the way to visit an apartment Mrs. Klein had just sold for way above market.

"I'd live in this area in a heartbeat if we could afford it," Mrs. Klein said, gazing out at the hilly, manicured lawns and old stone mansions. "It's the Bel Air of Hillsdale."

"Well, maybe after the divorce comes through . . . ," Whitney said. Haley could tell by the dreamy look on Whitney's face that she was imagining *all* the things they would do once Mrs. Klein's divorce from Jerry was complete, and she and her mom had what was rightfully coming to them.

For a while, it looked as if Mrs. Klein didn't stand a chance against Jerry's legal team. But then Mr. Klein's new girlfriend, Trish, had had a minor meltdown and threatened to leave unless Jerry whisked her off to the Caribbean for a few months. Since his lawyers could no longer seem to get in touch with him, his case against Mrs. Klein was growing weaker by the day.

Linda pulled up to a fancy condominium complex, which Haley instantly recognized as Sasha Lewis's former home. "Hey, didn't Sasha used to live here?" she asked, giving a glance to the front seat.

"Funny you should say that, Haley," Mrs. Lewis said as she parked the car and reapplied her bright red lipstick. "Because it's the Lewis condo I just sold. That place was starved for a woman's touch, but after I worked my magic, it sold in three days."

"No. Way." Whitney's eyes nearly popped. "So Sasha's dad is back from Atlantic City oblivion. Man, that guy is such a loser."

As if on cue, Mr. Lewis rapped on the driver's-side window.

Mrs. Klein giggled girlishly as she rolled down her window. "Hi, stranger," she said, smoothing out a few of her stray hairs. "So are you ready to hand off your keys to the new owner and take possession of *your* new life?"

That's weird, Haley thought. *Is she flirting with him?*

Linda Klein had always been a petite, peppy woman. After the initial separation from Jerry, Haley noticed she had let herself go a bit, but now she was back to her trim and toned self.

Linda popped out of the car and let Jonathan Lewis kiss her on both cheeks. She lingered for just a moment too long in his embrace before they headed upstairs to sign the final papers and turn over the condo.

There is definitely something going on between them, Haley decided. *I wonder how Whitney's going to take it when she finds out? My guess would be not well. Maybe I should just bring it up now.*

"So, um," Haley began, once the adults were out of earshot. "Do you think maybe there's something going on between your mom and Sasha's dad?"

"What?" Whitney practically screamed. "No, ew. Wouldn't it be, like, incest if they were . . . you know. I mean, Sasha and I used to be almost like sisters!"

"Notice the words *almost* and *like* in that

sentence, Whitney. You and Sasha were never actually related," Haley pointed out. "And would it be such a bad thing if your mom had a new man in her life? From what I've heard, losing custody of Sasha really got Mr. Lewis to turn his life around. Maybe he'll be good for your mom, now that he's sobered up."

"I don't even want to think about it," Whitney said, crinkling up her nose. "He's practically an ex-con."

At that moment, Mrs. Klein and Mr. Lewis emerged from the condo *holding hands.*

"Whitney," Mrs. Klein said, bursting into a grin. "We have something to tell you. Jonathan and I . . . well, we've grown close over the past few weeks. Very close. In fact, we've decided . . . after the divorce comes through . . . we've decided we want to live together."

Whitney was practically hyperventilating. "This. Is not. Happening."

"I'll talk to her," Haley said, taking Whitney by the arm and walking her into the lobby of the condominium complex.

"So what tipped you off?" Whitney asked, holding her stomach as she sat on one of the modern sofas in the lounge area.

"I don't know," Haley said. "Just the way they were looking at each other."

"I hate my life," Whitney said, laying her head down on the stiff arm of the sofa.

"Come on, it's not that bad," Haley said. "I'm sure

the divorce is hard on you. And it will be strange getting used to having a new man in the house—"

"Aren't you supposed to be helping?"

"Well, look at it this way. At least you know where your parents are most of the time. Mine have totally fallen off the planet."

"Haley?" Whitney asked, looking up.

"Yeah?"

"Can I tell you something?"

"Sure."

"I sort of took something from Mimi's Boutique," she confessed. And then, like a tightly sealed dam that had cracked wide open, the words suddenly flowed out rapidly. "Okay, it was more than just something. It was a lot of things. And not just Mimi's either. But I was planning on bringing it all back. It's not stealing if you don't plan on keeping it forever. Only, now I'm scared. What if I get caught?"

"Do you think they have you on surveillance videos?" Haley asked tentatively.

"I don't know. It's just, Principal Crum was lecturing us the other day. And I got to thinking, maybe he's talking about me. I didn't think I'd taken that much stuff, but then when I looked in my closet . . ."

Haley winced. "Okay, let's think about this," she said. "I'm sure Mimi's just wants the merchandise back. Maybe we should start there. You could turn yourself in to the store and explain, and maybe they wouldn't press charges."

"Do you really think so?" Whitney asked innocently.

"Maybe." Haley was pretty sure, though, that
Whitney was in way over her head.

● ● ●

Leave it to the Klein women to turn a regular old
Saturday afternoon errand into a soap opera. Here
Haley thought she was just hanging out with Whitney,
and instead she gets to witness Mrs. Klein's awkward announcement that Sasha's dad is her new boyfriend. And
then to top it off, Haley has to hear Whitney's confession about being the infamous Bergen County shoplifter.

If you think Whitney is a good person deep down,
and that Haley should help correct her mistakes, go to
page 220.

If you don't want Haley associating with the Klein
women, and believe Whitney's problem is too serious for
Haley to handle on her own, then turn Whitney in on
page 225.

Alternately, you can help Sasha Lewis try to reunite
her parents before Jonathan Lewis moves in with Mrs.
Klein and it's too late. For that scenario, turn to page 214.

Whoever thought Whitney would be the first of
Haley's friends to become a felon? But in this case, will
the punishment fit the crime?

INVESTIGATE WHITNEY

A bad reputation is the worst of all punishments.

Lately, Whitney Klein had been acting even more out-rageous than usual. For starters, she'd been coming to school with shopping bags full of brand-new clothes, most still with tags on them. Considering how few books she kept in her locker, it worked well as a makeshift closet. Throughout the school day, Whitney would periodically change her clothes, just to watch people's reactions to her new "scores."

Haley found it all very fishy. After all, Jerry Klein had supposedly cut up all his daughter's credit cards after receiving her "back to school" bill in the fall.

Mrs. Klein, meanwhile, had taken all her assets that weren't frozen and sold them to pay for her expensive divorce lawyers, Scott Winkler and Bob Balboa. Everyone knew Linda Klein had been reduced to living in the Floods, at least until after the divorce came through. There was certainly no way she could've afforded to keep Whitney in a constant rotation of new designer clothes.

And, as Haley recalled, it wasn't as if Princess Klein had ever thought to take an after-school job to make up for her lack of allowance.

So, Haley was fairly certain Whitney Klein was, or had something to do with, the Bergen County shoplifter she'd been hearing so much about. But before she did anything about it, Haley wanted to investigate, just to be certain.

She began by looking for clues online. Haley first patrolled Whitney's personal Web pages, since Whitney was known for taking pictures of herself every day and posting them on her home page. Haley compared Whitney's outfits in the photos with a list of items that had been stolen from Mimi's and other boutiques over the previous month. For nearly every garment listed, she found a photo match in Whitney's blog archives.

Exhibit A, Haley thought, dragging some of the JPEGS to her desktop and storing them in a digital folder labeled "The Secret Life of Whitney Klein." As she continued trolling, an instant message from

Annie Armstrong popped up on her computer screen.

A: How come I see more of your mom than you these days?

H: Has she changed her hair lately? We're starting to forget what she looks like over here.

A: They've just been superbusy with this big case. They're in our living room ALL the time. Which I don't mind. The guy your mom brought in from San Fran is so CUTE! Peter Benson = totally dreamy.

Haley raised an eyebrow. *What exactly is going on at Armstrong and White?* she wondered.

A: So have you asked your parents yet about going to Spain over spring break with Sebastian and me and Dave? You know it's just over a month away.

H: Not yet. I'm working up to it. Will update you shortly. Seeya.

Haley signed off, wondering just how late it would be that night before she heard her mother's car pull into the driveway. She couldn't exactly ask about the trip to Spain if her parents weren't in the house.

Though Haley was supposed to be investigating Whitney, she had a sudden feeling that the defendants weren't the only thing toxic about her mother's big case. ● ● ●

The evidence against Whitney certainly seems compelling. But what do you think Haley should do with it?

Have her offer to help Whitney out of her jam on page 220. Turn Whitney in to Principal Crum and the police on page 225.

Alternately, if you think other people's problems should remain just that—other people's problems—then have Haley start planning that spring break trip to Spain on page 228.

Finally, if you think there is nothing more intriguing than former supermom Joan Millers' current disappearing act, turn to page 233. Maybe you'll even discover why Haley's parents moved to New Jersey in the first place.

WHAT'S GOING ON

The truth isn't always easy to find.

Haley showed up at her mom's office determined to get some answers. Not only had both her parents completely forgotten her sixteenth birthday, but lately, they'd been leaving Mitchell entirely in Haley's care. Neither Joan nor Perry had been home to do more than shower and occasionally sleep in weeks.

Plus, thanks to Sebastian Bodega, Haley had an open invitation to go to Spain over spring break, with Annie Armstrong and Dave Metzger tagging along. She hardly felt the need to *ask* her parents' permission at this point, but she did need to at least let them know she was thinking of going, and make sure that someone would be around to watch Mitchell for the time she'd be away.

In the somewhat shabby reception area at Armstrong & White, Haley waited, and waited, and waited some more. Finally, her mother came out to see her. Well, limped was more like it. Joan had serious bags under her eyes. Her skin was sallow and dull from lack of sleep, and her hair was a tangled wreck.

"You look awful," Haley said, keeping her distance.

"We're under a lot of pressure," Joan said. "I know it may not seem like it to you, because this case doesn't have any direct bearing on your life, but we're doing something important here."

"Who's Peter Benson?" Haley asked.

Her mother sighed and poured herself a cup of black coffee. "Someone I worked with in San Francisco."

"And . . ."

"My old firm flew him out here with a few colleagues so that they could help out on our case. We never would have been able to pull this thing together without him and the others."

"So why are you and Dad sleeping in separate bedrooms?" Haley asked, narrowing her gaze.

"Because Peter had a thing for me in San Francisco. Nothing happened. But it made your father . . . uncomfortable. That's why we moved to New Jersey."

"Is anything happening now?"

"No." Her mother smiled faintly. "Look at me, Haley. We're all walking zombies here. I'm lucky if I can grab a few minutes of sleep, a shower and a meal every few days. I certainly wouldn't have time to start an affair."

"Well, do you want to? Start an affair with him?"

"Haley, I love your father very much. There's no one I'd rather be with. That will never change."

"Then why won't you come home?"

"I will. As soon as we're done with this case."

"Mitchell told me he's starting to forget what you look like."

"Haley, I—" Joan stopped herself. "I won't have worked all this time for nothing. I can't pull out now."

This was the hardest part of having a crusader like Joan Miller for a mother. Because Haley knew her mom's case had to be pretty critical for Joan to be killing herself like this to win it. And with the stakes so high, and the environment in peril, Haley felt guilty being the kid at home complaining of motherly neglect. Even if she had every right to be angry.

"Well, I just came to tell you Mrs. Lewis—did you know she's been treating Mitchell? Well, she thinks he's a mathematics savant. He can solve college-level problems, and he keeps asking for more. She wants to talk to you about putting him in a special school. That is, as soon as you have some time."

Joan choked back tears. "That's great. That's really great news."

"Oh, and I'm thinking of going to Spain for spring break. It's not for sure yet, but I'm considering it. Annie and Dave and Sebastian are all going.

We'd be staying with Sebastian's family, and there'd be chaperones. Of course we'd have to find someone to watch Mitchell, if you weren't finished up with your case by then and Dad was still working on the documentary. But don't worry, I'll take care of it, depending on what I decide to do."

Joan smiled weakly. "You're getting to be such a grown-up."

Haley looked back at her. "Well, I am sixteen now," she said. Haley watched her mother's face as the realization hit her. Joan had been so busy at work, she had forgotten her only daughter's sixteenth birthday.

"I'll make it up to you, Haley. I promise," Joan said, unable to look Haley in the face. She gathered her strength, got up and walked back toward the glass-enclosed conference room, leaving Haley alone in the reception area.

Haley watched as her mother approached an attractive young man. He stood up with a concerned look on his face as Joan broke down in tears, and then collapsed in his arms.

Well, I guess that's Peter Benson, Haley said to herself.

● ● ●

Haley's mother has never lied to her before, but that was a pretty intimate moment with Peter Benson that Haley just accidentally witnessed. Do you think

there's something going on between Mrs. Miller and her former coworker? Or is Haley being overly suspicious?

To have Haley go straight to her father and report what she saw, turn to page 252. If you think Haley should ask her mom who Peter Benson is, turn to page 233. Alternately, you can have Haley forget her family troubles and get started planning that trip to Spain with Annie, Sebastian and Dave on page 228.

Haley's family life has always been a source of strength. What will she do now that there's trouble in the house of Miller?

Play with fire, and you can get burned. Launch yourself through a flaming heart, and it might be over 80 percent of your body.

"You don't look so bad," Haley told Shaun as she stood at his bedside at the hospital. That wasn't exactly true. Shaun's head had a big bandage on it; he had cuts and scrapes on his face; and there were some pretty serious burns on his neck, hands, forearms and shins.

"Thank the stars for leather jumpers," Shaun said. "That skinny suit darn near saved my life. Docs said I would've been seared rare all over if I hadn't been wearing my gear."

"So how long is it going to take you to get better?" Haley asked.

"Durn, girl, I 'spect I'll be back on my motorbike next week."

"Seriously, are all your . . . parts okay?"

"Tip-top, 'cept for this here little section of my noggin." Shaun pointed to the bandage. "Doc says I bruised my olfactory bulb. All I know is, I can't smell or taste any of this bunk hospital food. Which is all right by me."

Haley tried to process what Shaun had just said. "You can't taste or smell *anything*?"

"Your auditory bulb bruised or something? I just told you that. Doc says it may come back, may not. Won't know until it happens. Or doesn't happen. Shoot, I can't keep all this ER honky-talk straight."

"Me either," Haley said and shivered. "I hate hospitals."

"Then hoss, why you here?"

"To visit your sorry self," Haley said. "Do you realize I had to walk here?"

"Your parents still MIA?" Shaun asked.

"Yup." Haley forced a smile, but it really was starting to get to her, always having to take care of Mitchell, rarely laying eyes on her mom or dad, doing all the household chores ever since Gam left to go back to Pennsylvania.

Shaun's nurse came in holding his chart. "All right, big boy, we've got to get you in for another CT scan."

"Alice, I love it when you sweet-talk me," Shaun said as the nurse raised the guardrails on his bed and wheeled him out of the room.

"See you in five, make that twenty," Shaun called out to Haley from the gurney. "Alice here's promised to take me down to see the hot tub in the physical therapy wing."

"Keep dreaming," the nurse said as Haley wandered down the hall to the waiting room. There, she found Irene Chen sitting alone, staring off into space. Haley walked over and quietly sat down beside her.

"He says you told him to do this," Irene said angrily.

"What?" Haley scoffed.

"He says it was your idea for him to do something dramatic to finally get my attention."

"Look, you're the one who asked me to talk to him about his eating binges and this whole professional eating kick he's been on lately. You had to know he was in love with you, and that he was only stuffing his face to get over the fact that you don't feel the same way about him."

"And your solution was to send him through a flaming heart at forty miles an hour?"

"Of course not! All I said was I thought he probably was only gorging himself because he couldn't have you. I told him to just go for it, and see if he had a shot."

"I'm never asking you for another favor again as long as I live."

"But he's crazy about you, Irene. I know you think you two are best friends and all, and that it doesn't matter, but you can't just ignore the fact that you're all he thinks about. It kills him every time you throw yourself at Johnny Lane. Who, by the way, is practically engaged to Sasha Lewis."

Irene folded her arms across her chest and frowned.

"Hey," Devon said, appearing in the waiting room. He walked over and kissed Haley on the cheek. "How's Shaun?"

"Well," Haley said, "it seems he may have lost his sense of taste and smell. For the time being, at least."

"Will that help or hurt his chances at becoming a professional eater?" Devon asked.

"That career choice may be on hold at the moment," said Haley.

"Did you know he was planning this?" Irene demanded.

"No way," said Devon. "He just kept saying his art project was going to be this big performance piece. I was expecting another Poseidon eating adventure. Do you think I would've let him do this if I'd known? I've already been all over the Troll about lighting the fuse on that contraption. Speaking of, I know this isn't exactly the best time to ask, but are either of you up for helping me with my art project later this week? Depending on the weather."

"I'll have to see how Shaun's doing," Irene said.

"Well, I'm in," said Haley. Irene glared at her. "What?" Haley asked. "I hate hospitals."

• • •

That was a close one. Shaun's hurt, but a few scrapes and burns and a bruised olfactory bulb is far better than never being able to walk again.

If you feel satisfied Shaun will make a full recovery, then go help Devon with his art project on page 236. If instead you think it's time to find out WHAT'S GOING ON with Haley's parents, send her to confront her absentee mom at the offices of Armstrong & White on page 201.

Wounds on the inside can be just as painful as the ones on the outside. Maybe it's time for Haley to let the healing begin.

PUSH IRENE'S BUTTONS

Never push a button without knowing what it's there for.

Haley's dad rolled in at dusk looking exhausted but glad to be home. Haley couldn't believe he was actually there in time for supper. Instead of making him cook, she suggested Chinese takeout for dinner. Perry gladly got back into the car to drive her and Mitchell up the hill to Golden Dynasty.

"Be back in a sec," said Haley as she hopped out of the family's hybrid SUV and left her dad and brother waiting in the parking lot.

Haley knew Irene would be working. Irene Chen was *always* working during the dinner hour. Sure enough, there she was at the hostess station, with the house phone stuck to her ear and a takeout ordering pad in front of her.

"Golden Dynasty, may I help you?" Irene asked as line two began to flash urgently. "Can you hold, please?" she said, answering the other line. "Golden Dynasty, please hold." Then line three flashed with another caller.

Irene looked at Haley and rolled her eyes. She put up one finger and asked her to wait a second. Then, during a pause between calls, she asked, "Are you the Buddha's Delight, shrimp with black bean sauce, steamed tofu, green beans, white rice, General Tso's chicken and egg rolls?"

"That's it," Haley confirmed, handing over several wrinkled bills from her dad's wallet. Haley wasn't sure why, but she felt compelled to add, "So, how about that daredevil stunt Shaun pulled last week? Pretty wild."

"It was too stupid for words," said Irene, waiting for the now-jammed cash register to open so that she could give Haley her change. "He's a fool."

"He's a fool for love," Haley said knowingly. "I didn't realize you set his heart on fire like that."

"What's wrong with this thing?" Irene said in an annoyed tone as she tried to pry open the drawer.

Dodging the subject once again, Haley thought and decided to press on.

"Oh, come on, you like him, too," Haley blurted out. "Don't act like you don't."

"Haley," Irene said seriously. "I don't."

"What are you, secret lovers?" Haley teased.

Just then, Haley noticed Mr. Chen standing stoically off to the right. He swooped in and started to reprimand Irene in Chinese. Haley couldn't understand a word he was saying, but she knew something was up.

"Thanks a lot," Irene said, pushing the bag of takeout toward her and handing over Haley's change out of her own pocket. "He thinks I have a boyfriend now, and that I've been lying to him all this time. In case you didn't know, I'm not even allowed to date."

As Irene followed her irate father into the kitchen, Haley realized she'd caused serious problems for her friend. She never should have pushed Irene so hard. Haley guiltily walked back to the car with a gut feeling that told her she probably wouldn't be seeing much of Irene Chen for a while.

● ● ●

In friendships, there are certain boundaries you just have to respect. Haley was out of line, and now Irene is the one who suffers.

Hang your head and go back to page 1.

REUNITE SASHA'S PARENTS

There's usually a good reason parents get divorced in the first place.

Haley entered the Sicilian Sun, a local Italian restaurant where she was supposed to be joining the Lewises for supper. It had been years since Mr. and Mrs. Lewis had seen each other, and Sasha had invited her closest friends to help break the ice.

What is she *doing here?* Haley wondered, staring at Linda Klein, who had wedged herself right in between Pascale and Jonathan.

"Haley!" Sasha, Johnny and Cecily greeted her warmly, looking relieved to see her. Clearly, there had already been some tense moments.

"Hi, everyone," Haley said, and sat down in the seat between Cecily and Sasha. It was an odd sensation being nervous for other people, so Haley did what she normally did when she was nervous: She started eating. Sasha passed her the bread basket, and she tore off a hunk of warm pumpernickel and slathered it with butter.

"Well, at least you're staying out of trouble these days," Pascale said to her ex-husband.

"I've really turned a corner," Jonathan said, looking at Linda affectionately. "Or I should say we've turned a corner."

I can't believe he just used the royal "we," Haley thought, unable to hide her horror. She couldn't think of a more awkward scenario than Whitney's mom showing up for Sasha's parents' first reunion in half a decade.

"Step by step," Linda Klein said, nodding her head.

"Silly me," said Pascale. "I thought recovering alcoholics were advised not to get involved romantically for a lengthy period of time, until their sobriety was firmly established."

The look on Sasha's face screamed "Help!"

"Linda's been good for me," Jonathan told the table. "She sold the condo for me last week. And she understands what I'm going through."

Guess Linda forgot to mention that she's not really an alcoholic, Haley thought. She knew Mrs. Klein only went to AA because it was basically like free therapy.

"It's a great time to sell in Jon's neighborhood," Linda explained, sipping her nonalcoholic drink through a cocktail straw. "But I do have to give some credit to my people who staged the apartment for me," she said, and winked in Haley's direction.

Her people? Doesn't she mean her illegal child laborers? Haley knew that Mrs. Klein had been using Whitney and her friends to help her sell houses on weekends, without even paying them.

"It's funny how putting up a little artwork and changing the furniture can make a house seem like such a nice place to live," said Linda.

"If only my dad would have thought to 'stage' the condo when I lived there," Sasha said sharply. Pascale smiled supportively, letting her daughter know that it was okay to confront her dad. Sasha seemed about to speak, then lost her nerve.

"Well, LK Realty handled the sale beautifully," Jonathan said, trying to steer the conversation back to a less controversial topic.

"Say," said Linda, looking at Haley, Cecily and Sasha as if she were about to bond with them. "Are you girls as into this SIGMA club as much as my Whitney is? It's some sort of volunteer goodwill organization, right? Like a resume builder for college applications."

"Sure," said Sasha. "That's *exactly* what it is." Haley and Cecily giggled.

"Since we're all here together," Pascale began, "there's something I'd like to discuss." Sasha sat up straight, bracing herself for talk of financial support or custody.

"I want Sasha to come with me to Paris," Pascale said. "I have a few loose ends I need to take care of. She has spring break coming up. It's an ideal time of year to go."

"Are you *serious*?" Sasha said, bursting with excitement.

"But the custody agreement isn't finalized yet," Jonathan started in. "You're not supposed to be able to take her out of the country."

"After everything you've done to Sasha," Pascale responded coolly, "are you really going to deprive her of her first trip to Paris?"

Sasha looked over at her dad and gave him a half smile. "No, I guess not," Mr. Lewis said, with a concerned expression on his face. Obviously, he was worried Pascale would drag Sasha off to Paris and never come back, and then he'd never see his daughter again.

"I thought maybe you could bring some of your friends," Pascale said to Sasha, then looked over at Jonathan. This seemed to be her way of appeasing him. If Sasha's friends came along on the trip, surely they'd all be returning to Hillsdale together.

Sasha was ecstatic. "Well, I want Johnny there, of course."

"I'll buy my lottery ticket tonight," Johnny joked optimistically. Sasha looked chastened by the fact that Johnny could never afford such an expensive trip.

"We'll figure something out," said Pascale. "Sasha, is there anyone else you'd like to join us?"

"Really?" Sasha asked, looking back at her mom. Pascale nodded. "Haley, Cecily, you in?"

Haley's stomach flipped. *A trip to Paris? In the springtime? Are you kidding?*

"Of course!" Haley and Cecily said in unison.

Haley was blown away by the thought of a Parisian spring break, but she also realized it would be a tough sell with her parents. Although . . . Haley suddenly wondered if she might not be able to take advantage of the fact that her parents were hardly ever at home these days, now that they had both become workaholics.

Maybe, she thought, *I'll be able to guilt my way into going on this trip.*

And with that, she started visualizing what she was going to pack.

● ● ●

The main course being served at the Sicilian Sun tonight: stress. No wonder Sasha needed backup.

But was Sasha's dad bringing his girlfriend to the family reunion really necessary? Or was that just his passive-aggressive way of handling an awkward encounter with his ex-wife? Should Sasha have confronted him about how he messed up their lives? And is that a crucial step in her process of moving on?

Wait until Whitney Klein hears about this one. What if . . . Jonathan Lewis and Linda Klein fell in love and got married? Would Sasha and Whitney survive as stepsisters?

If you think all Haley has on the brain is finding a way to make that trip to France possible, head home to propose the Left Bank to her parents on page 241.

If you think that mention of SIGMA was enticing, then go find Whitney and Coco and figure out what the next password is on page 244.

Paris in springtime, or gambling in Jersey. How can Haley go wrong?

GET HELP FOR WHITNEY

It's hard to turn your back
on a friend in need.

Right around the time Mimi's Boutique installed a new surveillance system, Haley had staged her own investigation into the recent shoplifting problem in Bergen County. She figured out pretty quickly that Whitney Klein was the culprit. Now all she needed to do was find a way to help her.

After all, it wasn't as if Whitney was a hardened criminal who needed to be locked up in a cell to learn her lesson. Stealing was a compulsive behavior, and probably helped her feel as though she were in control of a life that right now was extremely out of control, thanks to her parents' messy divorce, the fact that her soon-to-be-stepmonster, Trish, was barely older than she was, and that her mother was shacking up with Sasha's alcoholic, gambling-addicted dad.

Or at least that's how Pascale Lewis, Hillsdale's newest child psychiatrist, had explained it.

With Sasha's mother's help, Haley got Whitney to return all the clothes to the stores and turn herself in to the police. Most of the items were either unused or worn only once for a short period of time, so everyone took everything back.

After Pascale clarified the situation for the shopkeepers, all of them agreed not to press charges—just so long as Whitney entered intensive therapy, and promised never to "shop" in their stores again.

That wasn't the only help Pascale offered. She knew that Linda Klein couldn't afford to pay her usual hourly therapy rate, at least not until the Kleins' divorce went through. So, since Whitney "used to be an old friend of Sasha's," Pascale took her on as a pro bono patient.

"Wow, Haley. I can't believe you totally fixed everything," Whitney said after the police called to say her case had been closed. She and Haley were grabbing coffee at Drip.

"Well, Sasha's mom was really the one who fixed everything," Haley said as she put sugar in her decaf latte. "But thanks."

A slight, pale freshman named Ryan McNally

reached past Haley and grabbed the sugar. He turned to the other freshman he was with, a chubby boy with braces and dark curly hair, and said, "Look, Ralph, as soon as I do this podcast with Dave Metzger, I'm going to get a lot more calls with work. I need a right-hand man who can mow lawns, churn out term papers, and who knows how to unclog a toilet. Tell me, am I talking to the right guy?"

Ryan, Haley knew, made a killing after school, taking on all the odd jobs and homework assignments Hillsdale High students had to do to keep their allowance flowing. Ryan took a percentage and then did all the work himself, leaving everyone happy and with cash in their pockets.

"Hey, what are you up to this weekend?" Whitney asked Haley. "Coco says there's a SIGMA somewhere. Supposedly, it's boys-only this time, since Spencer has to lie low on account of his mom's campaign for senator and all."

"Isn't Mrs. Eton running for *governor*?" Haley asked.

Whitney, unfazed, continued. "They're not letting *anyone* in except the original five founders. So I think Coco and I are gonna crash it. Wanna come?"

"Um, I guess," Haley said absently. She was now too busy staring at the gorgeous couple walking toward them wearing sunglasses and carrying guitar cases to pay much attention to Whitney. As the couple got closer, Haley realized it was Sasha Lewis and Johnny Lane.

They must have just finished practice, Haley thought, recalling that Sasha had recently joined Johnny's band, the Hedon, as a guitarist and lead vocalist. Sasha and Johnny seemed to be getting closer and closer as a couple these days. Sasha had even told Haley that she was bringing Johnny, along with a few other friends, on a trip to Paris with her mom over spring break. The way Sasha had said it made Haley think she had an open invitation to go.

"Hey," Haley said, smiling at the golden couple. That is, until she saw the cross looks on both Whitney and Sasha's faces. Sasha brushed by them without saying hello, and Johnny shrugged and followed his girl out the door.

That's when Haley remembered that Whitney's mom was now dating Sasha's dad. Which had to be awkward for everyone.

And to complicate matters further, Sasha's mom was the one who had just helped keep Whitney out of a juvenile detention center.

The drama, Haley thought, her head swimming. *Oh, the drama.*

● ● ●

That was certainly a close call at Mimi's Boutique. If Haley hadn't intervened in the shoplifting scandal, Whitney could've gotten into real trouble. But is she out of the woods just yet? Will Whitney's friendship with Sasha ever be repaired? And could they potentially end up as sisters someday?

If you think Haley should get in on those Paris plans for spring break, have her ask her parents' permission on page 241.

If you think crashing a boys-only poker game sounds like more fun, have Haley team up with Whitney and Coco on page 244.

Finally, have Haley go sit in on Ryan McNally's podcast at Dave Metzger's on page 248.

TURN HER IN

**People just love to shoot
the messenger.
In the back.**

Haley noticed a flyer that said SHOPLIFTER WANTED ALIVE—REWARD hanging on the bulletin board outside the school nurse's office. She could tell from the handwriting that Dave Metzger had designed it, and she also recognized the number printed on the bottom. Everyone recognized that number. It was the Ryan McNally hotline.

Ryan was a pale, slight freshman at Hillsdale High who had made a killing getting paid to do other students' dirty work. In exchange for a portion of your allowance, Ryan would mow your lawn, babysit your younger siblings, do dishes, clean out your garage and even finish your homework. No job was too menial or too hard, and everyone came out ahead.

Haley took a closer look at the poster. In fine print, it advertised witness-protection services for any student who came forward with information about the shoplifter or shoplifters. Haley had no doubt in her mind that Ryan had figured out some ingenious way to get the local boutiques to pay him to help solve the crime.

It presented a difficult dilemma for Haley. She knew she had gathered more than enough evidence to prove Whitney was the guilty party, but she was still uncertain how best to proceed. *I don't really want to be the one to rat her out,* Haley thought, unable to make herself march right down to Principal Crum's office and turn the information over to him.

The Ryan McNally hotline, on the other hand— that was easy to call.

Once Ryan was tipped off to Whitney's criminal activity, he set up a sting operation and nabbed her red-handed. He got a cash payout from the stores in the low four figures. And Haley got to keep some of the stuff Whitney stole.

However, Ryan's witness-protection program wasn't quite as reliable as some of the other services the freshman offered. Soon, the whole school knew that it was Haley Miller who had turned Whitney in.

Even though Whitney Klein had been in social

purgatory when she was caught, no one at school wanted to see the former teen queen in lockdown at a juvenile detention center.

Haley was ostracized. Her social life was over. And the worst part was, the clothes Whitney had stolen didn't even fit.

● ● ●

Hang your head and go back to page 1.

PASSPORT TO PARADISE

Some problems are just impossible to shake, even if you leave the country.

On the day Mrs. Armstrong convinced Mrs. Miller to let Haley go to Spain, Haley and Annie sprinted over to the passport agency together. They filled out all the proper documents—except the ones requiring parental signatures—and had their photos taken. Haley's, of course, came out looking atrocious. But what did she care? She was going to Spain!

"Do *not* let me forget to pick up Mitchell at therapy later," Haley said. "I know my mom is never going to remember. I cannot wait for this case to be over so our lives can go back to normal again."

"I don't know," said Annie. "I think it's kind of nice not having my mom constantly monitoring my every move. And did you notice how easy it was to get permission to go to Spain? It's a *foreign country*. And we're going *with boys*. My mom didn't even ask about the room situation. Can you believe it?"

"Isn't this just going to be the most amazing trip *ever*?" Haley said enthusiastically. "We're going to Seville! With Sebastian as our guide!"

"Oh, tell me about it," said Annie. "Ten whole days without Hannah Moss constantly pestering us. I can hardly wait."

Ever since Hannah had horned in on their Spanish group and gotten friendly with Annie's boyfriend, Dave Metzger, Annie had felt threatened. No matter how many times Dave reassured Annie that nothing was going on between him and Hannah, Annie still couldn't help but be suspicious. Not to mention annoyed at all of Hannah's precocious little habits.

"It'll be just like it was before she joined our Spanish group," Annie said with a sigh of relief.

Haley, meanwhile, felt an ache in the pit of her stomach. "Um, so I guess Sebastian didn't tell you then."

"Tell me what?" Annie asked.

"Don't be angry, Annie," Haley replied. "But since everyone else in our Spanish group was already going, Sebastian went ahead and invited Hannah too."

Annie's face went white. "But we already finished our Seville project!" she blurted out. "What was he thinking?"

"Well, these recruiting meetings with college swimming scouts have gotten him worried about his grades. I think he made a deal with Ms. Frick. We can all get extra credit for the year if our Spanish group comes back and does another presentation for the class. Which will be a cinch, actually. I'm bringing my video camera to film *everything*."

Annie stormed out of the passport office in a huff, bumping right smack into Hannah Moss in the parking lot. "You," she seethed at Hannah.

Haley had assumed Hannah would be just as thrilled as she was to be going to Spain, but instead, Hannah looked positively depressed. "Are you okay?" Haley asked.

"I can't go with you guys," Hannah reported, bursting into tears and holding out her passport. "I might as well have not even gotten this. My parents said no this morning. They think I'm too young to go."

Annie's face curled into a Cheshire cat grin.

Haley looked down at Hannah's picture on her passport and then read her birth date. "You're only *thirteen*?" Haley gasped.

"What? Let me see that!" Annie demanded. "So does that mean you skipped . . . two grades?" Annie's jealousy over Dave had instantly morphed into jealousy over Hannah's accelerated academic standing.

"I'll be fourteen in May," Hannah said.

"Why didn't you tell us?" Haley asked.

"I didn't think you guys would want to be friends with me if you knew I was so much younger than you. And you're the first real friends I've ever had."

"Come on, kid," Haley said protectively. "Let's go to Drip. I'll buy you a cup of coffee, and you can tell me all about it. Um, on second thought, better make that hot chocolate. I wouldn't want to stunt your growth or anything." Hannah smiled.

At the coffee shop, Coco De Clerq and Whitney Klein were monopolizing the best booth. "If it isn't the nerd herd," Coco said as Haley, Hannah and Annie walked in.

"Whatever, Coco," Annie said without missing a beat. "Everyone knows you're lower on the social totem pole than we are at this point. One of you's got sticky fingers, and the other can't hold her liquor. I heard Spencer even took you off the SIGMA list."

"Well, that shows how much you know," said Whitney. "He took *everybody* off the SIGMA list. It's only the founders now. Spencer can't get caught gambling or it'll ruin his mother's senatorial campaign. So there."

"Mrs. Eton is running for governor, Whitney," Coco corrected her.

"Same difference," Whitney said, rolling her eyes.

And to her, Haley realized, it actually was. As far as Whitney was concerned, Mrs. Eton might as well have been running for chancellor of America.

"Anyway, Coco and I are crashing," Whitney added.

"Yeah, that's a way to restore your image," Annie

cracked. "Start crashing parties with all the un-invited losers."

"Come on, Whitney," Coco said, grabbing her arm. "We're getting out of here."

● ● ●

Well, the good news is, Haley got the "yes" from her parents just in time to get her passport ready for Spain. The bad news is . . . well, there really isn't any downside at this point.

The trip to Spain to visit Sebastian's family should be a pretty laid-back one. Especially since Hannah Moss won't be there to antagonize Annie. The only foreseeable problem will be traveling with Haley's neurotic friends, Annie and Dave. On second thought, maybe she should reconsider going on this trip after all.

To join Coco and Whitney as they crash the STAG SIGMA, turn to page 244.

If you think Haley should spend some quality time with Annie and Dave before she makes up her mind, head to Dave's house to observe his podcast with Ryan McNally on page 248.

Finally, how much do you think it matters that Haley pick up Mitchell at therapy? Care to find out? Turn to page 255 to see what happens when Haley stops filling in for her mother.

WHO IS PETER BENSON?

Even guilty people are afforded the presumption of innocence.

It took some doing, but Haley finally cornered her mother in the driveway one morning before Joan could slip away to the office. At first, Haley just peppered her with a few simple questions about the toxic torts case. Then she moved on to a tougher line of questioning about "this Peter guy."

Her mother gave only brief, terse answers, which frustrated Haley even more than if Joan had said nothing at all. Still, Haley pressed even harder, but the more she quizzed her mother, the quieter Mrs.

Miller became. Finally, Joan just reminded Haley to pick up Mitchell at therapy after school, got in her car and drove off.

Haley was desperate. She decided she had to take matters into her own hands. Even though it made her uncomfortable, she began to invade her mother's privacy. She snooped through the files in her parents' bedroom and pawed through the top drawer of Joan's dresser, looking for clues of any sort that might lead her to some answers.

Over the course of the next week, Haley gathered together a pretty clear picture of who "Peter Benson" was. She searched online databases for info about his past. He was Northern California born and bred. His parents owned a vineyard. Haley was also finally able to put together how Peter and her mother had met. It seemed they had overlapped for one year at Stanford Law School.

But Haley still didn't have the information she really wanted. What she needed to know was whether her mother's relationship with Mr. Benson was purely professional, or if something romantic was brewing between them.

Just the possibility of an affair made Haley's stomach ache. So when Annie Armstrong called and invited Haley to listen in on Dave Metzger's next podcast, the offer sounded more than a little appealing.

All the snooping seems to be disagreeing with Haley. She's just not cut out for sneaky deception.

If you think Haley should trust her mom and drop the Peter Benson investigation, then send Haley over to Dave Metzger's house for his next podcast on page 248.

If you think something's going on between Haley's mother and this Peter Benson character, have Haley go straight to her father and talk to him about it on page 252.

Finally, if you're sick of Haley always getting stuck filling in for her mom, find out what happens if she doesn't pick up Mitchell from his therapy appointment on page 255.

THE PERFECT STORM

Beauty is everywhere, even amidst destruction.

For weeks, Devon had been watching the weather reports religiously, awaiting a very precise alignment of meteorological conditions. For his art project, he needed it to be stormy enough to produce a lot of precipitation, but warm enough so that the rain didn't turn to sleet or snow.

The reason for all this careful planning? He wanted to photograph his neighborhood, the Floods, but only after a *real* flood had taken place.

Just as he was about to give up and change tactics, the local news team predicted heavy thunderstorms for a midweek afternoon. Sure enough, right on cue, as Haley and Devon pulled out of the Hillsdale High parking lot in his jalopy convertible, dark storm clouds rolled in. They drove to the edge of the Floods and parked on high ground. Then they put the convertible top up and suited up in their army green oilskins before hiking down into the valley.

While they waited for the rains to come, Haley tried to make conversation. "So. What do you have planned for spring break?" she asked.

"Well, Shaun's parents are hosting their art exhibition for all Mr. Von's students. So I'll probably spend some time over there. And then just taking care of my little sister."

"Yeah. Me too. I mean, I bet I'll be watching my younger brother. Either that, or going to Paris with Sasha Lewis and her mom. Or Spain with Annie Armstrong, Dave Metzger and Sebastian Bodega. I can't really decide."

Devon chuckled. "Popular girl. I bet Paris would be beautiful this time of year," he said. "So would Spain." It wasn't exactly the reaction Haley had been hoping for. She wanted Devon to beg her to stay in Hillsdale with him and hang out, maybe even introduce their younger siblings on a playdate.

They sat there in awkward silence until the rain started to come down in sheets. Puddles almost instantly began to dot the parking lot they were standing in. "Finally!" Haley exclaimed.

"Just wait until one of these storm drains clogs,"

Devon said, snapping away on his 35mm camera. "Then we'll be in business."

Within the hour, that's exactly what had happened. At first, the water just skimmed Haley's ankles. But soon, it was rushing past her knees. "Is this dangerous?" Haley asked as they climbed onto the roof of a half-submerged red pickup truck, and hopped to the roof of another vehicle.

"Nah," Devon said as Haley hurried to keep up, schlepping his camera bag around and opening box after box of film for him, all the while trying to protect it from the rain.

"Although this *is* the highest water level I've ever seen," Devon said, snapping a shot of a sunken grocery cart, then moving on to a Stop sign that was half underwater, half out. Next it was playground equipment rising up from the gray river running through the Floods.

As they crossed a small bridge, Haley's eyes widened. House after house had been washed out or breached by the floodwaters. Haley gave Devon a fresh roll of black-and-white film, and he captured an old bearded man sitting in a rocking chair up on his now-muddy front porch.

Haley wondered how the man could be so stoic, when clearly he'd just lost most of his possessions. She felt strange helping Devon record the moment, and found herself looking away.

Above the sound of rain, Haley heard the faint sound of mewing. "Did you hear that?" she asked, but Devon was busy setting up his next shot. Again, Haley heard the mews. This time Devon looked up too. He listened for a second, then marched off into the woods, leaving Haley to watch out for all the equipment. Devon returned moments later carrying two baby kittens. One was a tabby; the other was gray and white.

"They're lucky little guys," Devon said, handing the shivering kittens over to Haley. "I found them in a cardboard box that somehow managed to stay afloat."

"We should get them inside," said Haley.

"But where?" Devon asked. "I can't keep them. My parents would kill me."

"And I can't take them. Our dog, Freckles, would kill them."

They both looked at each other, instantly understanding exactly what the other was thinking. "What time is he coming home from the hospital?" Haley asked.

Devon looked at his watch. "We just might make it." They grabbed their stuff and headed straight for Shaun's.

● ● ●

How cute is Devon? He's an artist. He rescues kittens. Haley is one lucky girl.

Then again, she just spent the entire day working without pay as his photo assistant. Would Devon be generous enough to return the favor if Haley asked him for help on one of her art projects? Or is he too much of a loner to care?

To send Haley and Devon to deliver the kittens and witness SHAUN'S TRIUMPHANT RETURN, flip to page 258.

If you think Haley should forget Devon and go with Annie, Dave and Sebastian to Spain, turn to page 271.

Finally, before you accept Sasha's invitation for that Paris trip, have Haley ask her dad for permission on the following page.

The best possible word a parent can say to a child: "Yes."

Haley closely studied her dad's behavior that evening as he got home from work and settled in. She wanted to make sure she picked the ideal moment to pop the spring break question. She knew she had only one chance to ask permission to go to Paris, and she refused to blow it on bad timing.

Perry came downstairs and opened the refrigerator. He took out a soft ripened cheese and poured himself a glass of red wine.

Once he finishes half that glass, I'll make my move, Haley decided, hiding in plain sight with her nose deep in *Brave New World*—assigned reading for her honors English class.

"So, Dad," she began casually as his wine reached the half-full point. "I have something to ask you about. I wanted to wait until you and Mom were both here together, but that seems like a lost cause, and spring break is just around the corner. You see, there's this trip—"

"The answer is yes," Perry said, leaning back in his chair.

"But you haven't even heard my question yet," Haley warned.

"Whatever it is you're asking me, the answer is yes, you can go. You deserve it, Haley. You've been stuck here taking care of Mitchell for weeks. I've noticed how much of the load you've been carrying, all the cooking, the cleaning, and that on top of your schoolwork. Really, wherever it is you want to go, it's fine by me. Unless, of course, you're planning to head to some war-torn region or country the U.S. doesn't formally recognize. But otherwise, have a blast."

"You spoke with Mrs. Lewis," Haley said, smirking.

"Yesterday, when I picked up Mitchell. You can use some of my frequent-flyer miles to pay for the ticket. Sounds like a fun trip. I know Reese is looking forward to it."

Haley looked at her dad, unsure of whether to shake him and demand what he'd done with her real father, kiss him for confirming that Reese Highland was definitely on board for the Paris excursion, or call Sasha and freak out in celebration. She decided the last was probably her safest bet.

● ● ●

A trip to Paris in springtime? And Reese Highland is coming? Oui oui, mon cheri. This sounds like a spring break to remember.

But there could be one glitch in those Left Bank plans. Johnny Lane still needs a ticket. If he can't come to Paris, will Sasha call off the whole trip? Have the kids pull together to help him out on page 262.

Who cares about Reese Highland in France when you can visit Sebastian Bodega in Spain? If you think Haley would rather jet off to a different part of Europe with Sebastian and the rest of her Spanish group, turn to page 271.

Finally, if staying in Hillsdale sounds more relaxing than boarding an international flight, find out what the artsy stragglers Shaun, Irene and Devon are up to on page 274.

Stag parties are no place for girls.

Spring was in the air and suddenly it seemed as if everyone in Hillsdale had coupled off. Even the wee'un from Haley's Spanish class, Hannah Moss, seemed to have found not one but two boys to spend her time with. Haley had seen Hannah hanging out with Dale Smithwick, the basketball team's skinny, shy, bespectacled manager, and also with freshman entrepreneur Ryan McNally, who had rigged up his own gold mine by doing chores and homework for other students in exchange for a percentage of their allowance.

Ugh, Haley thought, watching as Hannah and Ryan chuckled over a salad in the cafeteria. *If they can find love, why can't I?*

Lately, it seemed as though all she ever did on Saturday nights was film Mitchell, answer e-mails and read her friends' blogs. Her only prospect for doing something more exciting was a recent invite from lame-o Annie Armstrong to join her, Dave and Sebastian Bodega in Spain for spring break. But that was still a couple weeks off. When Haley received a text message from Coco De Clerq asking her to help crash an all-boys SIGMA that Saturday night, it was undeniably a better option than anything else on the table.

Haley arrived at the De Clerqs' mansion in an all-black ensemble, just as Coco had requested. She found Coco and Whitney, also dressed in black, upstairs in Coco's bedroom. "The boys in our grade are lame," Coco said bitterly as she grabbed Haley's video camera and flung herself onto her down comforter. "I mean, grow up. They can't just suddenly cut us out of SIGMA and make it founders-only. I don't care if Spencer's worried about getting caught doing something shady during his mom's campaign."

"Members-only was only fun when we were members," Whitney added, sitting in front of Coco's oversized mirror and experimenting with her friend's huge collection of high-end cosmetics.

Coco struggled with the video camera, looking for a power button. "It's the red one," Haley explained.

"I knew that," said Coco, smiling fakely and pointing the lens toward her own face. "Hello, and welcome to another day in the life of Coco De Clerq. I'm here with Whitney Klein, professional makeup artist and style guru. Whitney, where do *you* think Spencer and his friends are holding SIGMA tonight?" She angled the camcorder toward Whitney, who was applying way too much red lipstick to her puffed-out pout.

"Well . . . ," Whitney said, concentrating really hard.

Coco, you'd be better off just calling your sister's cell phone and asking. Spencer's probably with Ali somewhere right now getting high, Haley thought, though she figured it was best not to share this thought.

"Maybe it's at . . . Matt Graham's?" Whitney said. "I saw him buying six bags of chips at the grocery store last night." With the pounds of makeup she now had on her face, Whitney exemplified the old saying "All done up with no place to go." At least not yet, anyway.

"Hmmm . . . Matt Graham's. Interesting thought. I'll get right back to you." Coco set the video camera down and marched over to her computer. Some months back, she had cracked the code to Spencer's e-mail, though she had only ever used it to monitor his dating life. Now she quickly scrolled to Spencer's log-in page, typed in his password and, after his e-mail in-box popped up, did a search for *Matt* and/or *Graham* in incoming or outgoing messages. "Ugh, my sister is such a slutbag," Coco said, noticing an e-mail headline from Ali in Spencer's queue. It read, "Wanna meet up late night?"

"Bingo," Haley said, looking over Coco's shoulder at an e-mail from Toby entitled "Founders Day," which specified the details of the next SIGMA party. "SIGMA's at Matt's tonight. The invite says, 'Bring your beers. Bring your cards. Bring your money. But don't bring your beeyotches. Boys only.'"

"Awesome!" Whitney exclaimed, running back over to the mirror to touch up her makeup. "Matt Graham totally has a thing for Haley. There's no way he won't let us in."

Haley wasn't quite sure if that was true or not. But then, what else were they going to do? Watch Whitney reapply her makeup all night?

● ● ●

Most people don't like to show up where they're un-invited, but Coco doesn't seem to have a problem with it. If you think Haley should follow the leader and crash the boys-only SIGMA party, go to page 265.

If you think Coco's crashing SIGMA is only going to further damage her already-bruised reputation, then have Haley TALK COCO DOWN on page 268.

Finally, if that trip to Spain sounds like a more appealing option, even if it is with the geek squad, send Haley off to start packing on page 271.

Puberty destroys a boy, then rebuilds him in a new image, albeit with a much different voice.

Dave switched on the podcast feed. He put his finger up in the air and then lowered it slowly as they went live. "Good morning, folks," he crooned into the mike. "Welcome to 'Inside Hillsdale.' We have with us today the freshman robot, the chore angel, Mr. Cleaner, the guy behind the cleanest bedrooms in town. He tackles household duties in a single bound. There is no lawn he cannot tame, no floor he cannot shine, and no mother he cannot fool into thinking her child spent the afternoon polishing the silver.

There is no better way to brownnose, folks, than to hire Ryan and let *his* hands get dirty. Ladies and germs, Ryan McNally."

"Hiya, Dave," Ryan said into the mike.

Annie, Hannah Moss and Haley were sitting on Dave's bed watching the podcast intently. Ever since Haley and Annie had figured out that Hannah was really only thirteen, and that she had skipped a couple grades to reach the sophomore class, they felt a sudden fondness for her.

"Ryan, tell us. What was the biggest mess you've ever come across?" Dave asked, opening the show.

"I've seen many a mess, Dave. A few houses that literally could have been condemned," Ryan said. "But I have to say, the morning after a Richie Huber house party typically brings the most disastrous interiors I'll see on the job. I once had to refinish his dining room table in forty-eight hours, because his parents were coming into town for a visit. That was not fun."

"I bet you've tackled some pretty sticky floors in your day," Dave said.

"I find the chemistry of it all just fascinating. Beer, for instance, turns into a positively gluelike substance when it dries on tile or linoleum. But I've made my own solvents to handle that."

"I heard," Dave read from the blue note cards on his desk, "that you once had to replace a stained glass window. Is that right?"

"After a Halloween party that shall remain name-less, yup," Ryan admitted. "Someone hurled a floor lamp through it."

"It's not a party until the floor lamps are flying. We're going to have to pause now for a brief word from our sponsors." Dave flipped to the next card. "This weekend in rock," he read, his voice rising, "Sasha Lewis makes her debut as the Hedon's newest member." Dave tried clearing his throat as his voice suddenly cracked into a high-pitched squeal. He tried again. "They're playing at the Station. Tickets are fifteen dollars." His voiced cracked even higher.

Haley held back her laughter. She knew they were broadcasting live, but she couldn't help it. The thought of Dave's voice cracking on air was *hilarious*.

Annie, meanwhile, looked away and began fiddling with her hair. Clearly, she was tense and anxious for her boyfriend, who grimaced and flipped on a previously recorded advertisement for Ryan's cleaning services: "Is your room a disaster zone? Does it seem like your lawn is growing faster than you can mow it?"

Hannah looked disappointed, probably because Dave's Proust questionnaire was always her favorite part, and now it looked as if the show wouldn't go on. *Maybe she's got a crush on Ryan,* Haley suddenly thought as she watched Hannah tentatively approach Ryan and ask her own set of questions. *They would sort of make a cute couple, seeing as they're both so little. Plus, Ryan's closer to her age.* Haley resolved to talk to Ryan about keeping Hannah company over spring break. Hannah was bound to be lonely since Haley, Annie, Dave and Sebastian would all be in Spain on holiday.

Over at the podcast table, Annie was making Dave gargle with warm saltwater as she gently massaged his throat. Haley wondered if this latest Dave/Annie drama would become the sole topic of conversation on their trip. She certainly hoped not.

● ● ●

What happened? Dave's usually such a smooth operator. A podcast host knows his voice is his bread and butter. So what has Dave cracking up? Isn't it a little late for him to hit puberty?

Hannah Moss has a crush on Ryan McNally. But will the enterprising frosh break her thirteen-year-old heart?

If you think Haley should get packing for Spain with the heady crowd, flip to page 271.

If you're more curious about Sasha Lewis's big debut gig with the Hedon, which Dave mentioned on-air, go check out the band's newest addition on page 262.

**If you expect your parents
to trust you, you have to
trust your parents.**

Haley dialed her dad's cell phone number frantically. "Hello?" answered Perry. He sounded surprised to have his daughter calling him during normal business hours.

"Dad," Haley said in a panic. "I need to talk to you. What do you know about this Peter Benson guy?"

There was a long pause. "How did you find out about Peter?" he asked.

"So there *is* something going on between them!" Haley gasped. "Mom's been acting so weird, I just did a little research. Did you know they were at Stanford at the same time?"

"No. I didn't," he said sharply. "Why wouldn't she tell me something like that? Look, Haley, I'll see you at home later. Keep an eye on Mitchell." Perry cut off the conversation.

Haley did as she was told and looked after Mitchell. Later that night, after she had put her brother to bed and drifted off to sleep herself, she was awakened by shouting from downstairs. Haley sat up in her bed. She listened to the name Peter Benson being screamed in every other sentence out of her dad's mouth. She even heard a few curse words exchanged, which she believed categorized this as the worst fight in her parents' eighteen years of marriage.

Five minutes into the shouting match, Haley got a text message.

"Everything okay?" It was from Reese.

The whole neighborhood must be hearing this, Haley realized, knowing it was unlike Reese to text her at night. She answered quickly.

"They're just having another one of their 'discussions,' " she wrote back.

"Can we do anything?" Reese asked. "It hasn't gotten violent, has it?"

We? she thought. *Violent?* Haley knew immediately that Mr. and Mrs. Highland must be sitting right next to Reese, and that they were likely the ones who had put him up to contacting her.

It wasn't just that the whole town heard about the Millers' fight by the end of the following day. Or that rumors started flying about spousal abuse and divorce.

Haley discovered from Annie Armstrong, who had talked to her mother, who had been clued in by Mrs. Miller, that even though Peter Benson and Joan had both been at Stanford, they had never actually met until two years ago when they started working together in San Francisco.

There really was nothing going on between them. Back in San Francisco, Peter had hoped there might be a chance for a relationship, but after Joan had explained that Perry was the man she loved most in the world, and that she would never, ever consider leaving her family, Peter had moved on. Now, he had a young fiancée waiting for him back in San Francisco, and romancing Joan was the last thing on his mind.

He had only come to New Jersey because it seemed like an opportunity to establish real environmental precedent, and Joan needed help on the case.

Whatever problems Joan and Perry were having before were now multiplied tenfold. It took months of counseling to get them back to the place where they could even discuss the situation in civil tones again. Haley and Mitchell, unfortunately, were caught right in the middle.

● ● ●

Hang your head and go back to page 1.

MITCHELL'S MOMENT

You can't watch a child every moment of the day.

Haley was tired of chores. She was tired of always picking up milk and juice at the grocery store. Of making breakfast for Mitchell every day, and ordering takeout for him at night. And she most definitely was tired of always, always, always doing the dishes.

She loved Mitchell, but she wasn't ready to be a mom.

So, that morning, instead of leaving a stack of opened bills for her dad with the amounts circled in red, so that they would actually get paid, she didn't even bother with the mail. She left her mother three messages throughout the day, saying she wouldn't be able to pick up Mitchell at therapy, and that Joan or Perry would have to do it. *Besides,* Haley thought, *Sasha's mom has been wanting to talk with them about Mitchell's case.*

Instead of running errands, Haley took the afternoon off. She went to the movies, and ordered popcorn, soda *and* candy. There was something liberating about waltzing into a darkened theater alone. As she sat down in her comfy chair with her popcorn and drink, she felt as if she were entering her own little world. And Haley definitely liked the feeling of escape.

Ninety minutes later, she reemerged from the cineplex feeling refreshed. She turned her cell phone back on, and saw that she had missed *eight* calls. Half were from her mother. Two were from her dad. And two were from an incoherent Mitchell.

Joan evidently hadn't picked up her messages all day. It wasn't *entirely* Haley's fault that Mitchell was abandoned, left to sit alone in Pascale Lewis's waiting room for three hours, causing him to slip further and further into an unreachable state. She just should've made sure that *someone* had relayed the news to her mom that Mitchell needed a ride that day.

At home that night, Mitchell once again began talking to his imaginary friend, Marcus. "Marcus.

Never. Leaves me," he said in his robot voice when Haley tried to apologize.

She felt horrible about what she'd done. She loved her brother, and now he no longer trusted her. She knew things between them would never be the same.

● ● ●

Hang your head and go back to page I.

SHAUN'S TRIUMPHANT RETURN

Even "the Shaun" is subject to evolution.

As Haley worked on an art assignment, someone who strangely resembled the old cartoon character Mr. Magoo entered Mr. Von's classroom, wearing a pair of dark sunglasses and carrying a wooden cane. He walked over to the chair where Shaun used to sit, before he'd been hospitalized because of that debacle in the parking lot with the motorbike and the flaming heart. The Magoo boy had hair buzzed close to his symmetrical head. Haley looked more closely.

"Shaun?" she asked, barely recognizing him without his blond mullet. He also looked as if he'd dropped twenty pounds. The transformation was re-markable.

"Please, call me 'the artist formerly known as Shaun,'" he announced to the class.

The last time Haley had seen Shaun was on the day he'd come home from the hospital, still swaddled in bandages for all his scrapes and burns. As a welcome-home gift, Haley and Devon had brought him two kittens they had rescued during a storm in the Floods.

Irene, meanwhile, had refused to make even an appearance at the homecoming. She was still mad at Shaun for using that stupid parking-lot stunt as a way to prove his love for her. After keeping vigil day and night at the hospital, she had packed up and left the minute Shaun's doctors said he would, for the most part, be okay.

Even now that he was right there in front of her, Irene wouldn't look at Shaun. Instead, she continued focusing on a drawing in her black sketchbook.

"Welcome back," Mr. Von said to Shaun. "While I still can't condone your choice of medium for the most recent art project, I am heartened to see that you're okay and that you are once again here with us."

Irene tried to maintain her usual scowl, but Haley detected the signs of a smile creeping into the corners of her mouth.

"Yeah, glad you're back, bro," Johnny Lane said. "The Hedon's playing this week, and crowd surfing just wouldn't be the same without you."

Haley had heard about the concert. Tickets were fifteen dollars each, and part of the money was going toward paying Johnny's way to Paris. Sasha's mother, Pascale Lewis, was taking Sasha and a few of her friends. Haley had gotten the invite, but she wasn't sure if this was exactly the best time to duck out on her family.

Which was why an alternate spring break invitation, to go to Spain with Annie Armstrong, Dave Metzger and Sebastian Bodega, was equally troubling.

Dale Smithwick handed Shaun a jar of sticky adhesive goop. "We're making collages," Dale whispered. Haley took a pile of her magazine, newspaper and fabric strips and gave them to Shaun, while Mr. Von handed him a clean sheet of poster board.

"Awww," Shaun said. "You shouldn't have."

Shaun lovingly twisted off the top of the goop jar and lifted out the plastic brush-applicator. His nose began to twitch just like a rabbit's, and a look of celebration spread across his face. "Yee-haw!" he shouted. "I love the smell of rubber cee-ment in the morning. Ladies and gentlemen, I believe my sense of smell is returning!"

Haley was stunned. She knew Shaun had bruised his olfactory bulb when he'd crashed into that flaming heart after professing his undying love for Irene. The doctors had said there was basically a 50 percent chance he would never smell or taste again. So it wasn't quite a miracle that he could now faintly detect the scent of glue. But it was a start.

Haley looked over at Irene, who was now openly beaming at the news. In that moment, she had a funny feeling that Irene and Shaun's relationship might finally be about to change.

● ● ●

The artist formerly known as Shaun is back and better than ever. But will his new haircut and slimmer physique prompt Irene to fall for him?

To find out what the other kids in Mr. Von's class did for their final projects, and to have Haley present the spooky short film she made with Gretchen, Mitchell and Gam Polly, go to the open exhibition at Shaun's house over spring break on page 274.

If you think Haley would rather go see the Hedon play, turn the page.

Good music + good cause
= really good time.

The Hedon had practiced for weeks leading up to their gig at the Station, which was important for two reasons. For starters, it marked Sasha's debut with the band. And Haley had also heard that some of the proceeds from ticket sales were going to help Johnny pay his own way on a trip to Paris over spring break.

Sasha, her mother and a few of Sasha's friends were headed to the City of Lights for an entire week. Haley had been invited to go, and her parents had even said yes, but she was still wondering if maybe this wasn't the right time to go away, given her mom's big case, her parents' current troubles and Mitchell's recent progress in therapy.

Unbeknownst to Johnny Lane and the other band members, Irene Chen had secretly promoted the Hedon's show all week. Haley had seen her passing out flyers in the cafeteria, putting posters up in the boys' and girls' locker rooms, and wallpapering the bathroom stalls with the announcement. Irene even got Dave Metzger to plug the event on his podcast, "Inside Hillsdale," without charging his normal rate.

It seemed incredibly benevolent of Irene—heralding Sasha's debut with the Hedon, and helping Johnny get together the money to run off to Paris with her—when Sasha had been the one who had made it painfully clear to Irene that Johnny's heart was taken.

Irene had harbored a secret crush on Johnny for years, and Haley now wondered if maybe her support of Sasha was a signal that she was finally ready to move on.

In any case, Irene's efforts worked. The Station was packed. "The Hedon rocks!" Cecily yelled, standing next to Haley and Reese Highland in the middle of the sold-out crowd.

"Woaaaahhhhoooo!" Haley cheered and applauded as the stage lights dimmed. The sound of footsteps filled the stage behind the velvet curtain. "I'm so excited," Haley said, bouncing up and down. She couldn't wait for Sasha's big debut!

As the curtains parted, Johnny, Sasha, Toby and Josh appeared onstage, all dressed in the Hedon's signature white-collared shirts and slim black ties. Sasha, in particular, looked incredibly cool. The bass drum kicked in and throbbed. Sasha began to sing softly over the beats in her sultry alto voice. She seduced the crowd within seconds. Every one stared at her, hypnotized, held captive by her beauty, listening to her every breath.

Then Johnny slammed in on lead guitar. The whole band erupted in unison.

● ● ●

That was awfully nice of Irene Chen. She single-handedly made sure Sasha's debut with the Hedon was sold out.

So has Irene finally gotten over her crush on Johnny Lane? Or is she secretly more obsessed with him than ever? Has Irene become a love slave who will do anything to make sure he's happy? Or is she about to fall for someone else?

Find out by having Haley stay in Hillsdale for spring break with Irene, Shaun and Devon on page 274.

If you think there is no way Haley would miss the opportunity to jet off to France with Sasha and friends, including Reese Highland, go to page 279.

Your inner voice is what
keeps you from being
another sheep.

Haley had a sinking feeling as she and Whitney followed Coco through the bushes in Matt Graham's yard. She knew girls were not welcome at this particular SIGMA. And she knew Spencer wasn't exactly enthralled with Coco De Clerq or Whitney Klein at the moment, either. But still, since she hadn't exactly spoken up by now, she sort of felt it was too late to abort mission. They were, after all, already in their all-black stalker gear, with black grease wiped across their cheeks, kneeling in front of the Grahams' bay window. Now was not the ideal time to turn back.

The Grahams' tudor McMansion looked just like every third house on the street, Haley noticed as they gripped the stucco, wood and brick façade and snuck around to the back.

"Follow me," Coco whispered as they approached the media-room windows. "Busted, boys," she said quietly as they identified Spencer, Drew, Toby, Matt and . . . Reese Highland sitting around a poker table.

He's not a SIGMA founder! Haley thought.

"Glad you could come this time, Highland," said Spencer. "I was starting to think you were uptight."

"Well, poker with the guys is a little different from a flash mob boozefest," Reese responded. "If this was how SIGMA was every time, I'd say sign me up."

Coco crouched down and commanded, "Haley, camera on."

Haley panicked. *Okay, this is officially the worst idea Coco's ever had,* she thought, still following orders.

"So, let's get down to business," Drew said, dealing out a hand of cards. "Now that Coco's been deposed, who's the hottest girl in our class?"

"I'd hook up with Haley Miller," one of the guys volunteered.

Who said that? Haley wondered, craning her neck to get a better look. It sounded like Matt Graham's voice.

"I don't know. Haley used to be supercute," Reese said. "But then she started hanging around with the Cocobots." The guys laughed.

Coco, however, looked pissed. Unable to control

herself, she stood up to rap on the glass. Haley tried to pull her away from the window in time, but Coco was set on delivering one of her rants. "I heard that, you moron," she said, banging on the window.

"Surprise!" Whitney shouted, jumping out of the bushes and throwing her arms into the air for spirit sprinkles. "Gotcha!"

"Well, look what we have here," Toby said, opening the window and looking down at the three snoops. "I thought I heard rats in the bushes." Reese didn't even acknowledge Haley, but just shook his head and turned away.

Toby held out his hand, demanding the video camera, and Haley didn't even bother to protest. He hit Erase, wiping out not only the footage of the SIGMA stag party, but also all the work she'd done since Christmas. Then he tossed the camera back to her, and slammed the window closed before drawing the blinds.

This is going to be bad, Haley thought as they left the property. She could just hear what all the kids were going to say at school.

● ● ●

Hang your head and go back to page 1.

It's ultimately your decision whether or not you do what Simon says.

"We're not going to crash SIGMA," Haley objected with authority. Coco was just about to lead the charge over to Matt's house when Haley stopped her in her tracks. "This is stupid. The boys want to have a night on their own. Why don't we let them? We can figure out something fun to do for a girls' night."

"What are you talking about?" Coco said, rearing back haughtily.

"Come on, Coco. Let's not be *those girls*. Besides, hasn't your reputation suffered enough lately? What if we got caught?" Haley reminded her. "Trust me. If we invade a guys-only SIGMA, we'll just be embarrassing ourselves."

Coco paused. She recognized Haley's gaze was protective and sincere. "Okay, fine," Coco agreed, with mock exasperation. "Anyway, they should be the ones chasing after us, right?" she concluded, suddenly sounding like the old self-assured Coco once again. "I think we should start planning for spring break. Let's make it just girls this year. What do you two think of coming out to our house in Quogue?"

"Awesomeness," Whitney said. "Will we be able to work on our tans?"

They turned to look at Haley, awaiting her response. The problem was, Haley didn't quite know what to say. This wasn't exactly her only option on the table for spring break.

Sasha Lewis and her mother, Pascale, were taking a group to Paris, including Reese Highland and Johnny Lane, and Haley had been invited to come along.

Annie Armstrong, Dave Metzger and Sebastian Bodega were headed to Sebastian's hometown in Spain, and Haley had received an invitation to join them as well.

And finally, there was the possibility of staying in Hillsdale and going to an art festival with Shaun, Irene and Devon.

Haley's head was swimming. She knew she needed to make up her mind fast.

• • •

So what do you think? Is Coco becoming a better person? Is Haley finally part of her permanent inner circle? And does she now view Coco as one of her best friends?

Or is Coco only showering her with attention because Cecily Watson and Sasha Lewis aren't interested in being Coquettes anymore?

If you think it would be nice for Haley to have a five-star getaway in the Hamptons, have her head out to Long Island and get closer to Coco on page 282.

If you think the superficial video footage Haley has been shooting of Coco and Whitney's escapades is a waste of her artistic talent, have Haley stay home over spring break and put together a real reel. Haley can make her artistic debut on page 274.

Alternately, you can send Haley to Spain (page 287) or Paris (page 279) with friends.

Regardless of which locale she ends up in, Haley's in for a fun-filled break from school. It's up to you to figure out which vacation is the best fit.

**Packing tends to be a lot
easier when you don't wait
until the last minute.**

Haley put off packing for spring break until the night before she and Sebastian and Annie and Dave were leaving for Spain. She was just too excited to figure out what she was going to wear. There were too many guidebooks to read, potential itineraries to map out.

When she could put it off no longer, Haley finally put out all the clothes she thought she would need, given the climate and the length of their stay. *That'll have to do,* Haley thought. Besides, Sebastian had assured her that if she forgot anything, it wouldn't be a problem, since they made clothes, shoes and bathroom products in Spain, too.

There was a knock at her bedroom door. She opened it, and found both her parents and Mitchell standing in the hall.

"Happy belated birthday to you," her parents sang, holding an ice cream cake with sixteen candles aglow. "Happy belated birthday to you."

"Happy. Birthday. Haley," Mitchell flatly chimed in.

Haley hesitated before she blew out the candles. She wanted to make sure she made the best possible wish.

She looked at her parents' faces and then leaned in and extinguished the candles with one smooth puff of air.

"We're so very sorry, Haley," her mother said with a tear in her eye. "About everything."

"We blew it, Haley Boo," her dad confessed, using her elementary school nickname. He looked at his wife and put an arm around her. "But your mom's just finished her opening argument. The trial starts next week. I bet by the time you get home from Spain, the Miller household will be back to normal again."

"I promise I'll never take on such a grueling workload again, at least not until we hire about six more lawyers," Joan said sincerely. "And I promise to make it up to you. To you and Mitchell both."

"Well, the mint chocolate chip ice cream cake

and this trip to Spain are a pretty good start," Haley said with a smile.

Joan pulled a small package out from behind her back and handed it to Haley. It was an envelope full of Spanish pesetas. "Have a good time over there, and be safe," she said.

Haley wrapped her arms around her mom, her dad and Mitchell, squeezing her family tight. She suddenly was sad to be leaving them for a week, and felt an overwhelming urge to stay home.

● ● ●

What do you think Haley should do? Explore the Spanish countryside with her friends? Or stay in Hillsdale, close to Mom and Dad, and hit the local ART FESTIVAL with Irene, Shaun and Devon?

To go to Spain and use those pesetas, jump ahead to page 287.

To stay in Hillsdale, turn the page.

An appreciation of fine art
starts in the home.

"Extraordinary," a woman in heavy black-rimmed glasses and red matte lipstick commented as she circled Shaun's no-longer-flaming iron heart, which was positioned in the middle of his parents' modernist living room. Shaun's mom and dad, or the Willkommens as Haley now knew them, had graciously opened up their home for an art show of works by Mr. Von's students, inviting a selection of their quirky friends as well as gallery owners, art collectors and museum curators in from Manhattan.

"Who's that?" Haley asked Devon as they

watched the bespectacled woman survey the crafts-manship of Shaun's welding.

"She's an art critic for a magazine in New York," Devon explained.

Shaun, wearing his blackout shades and still car-rying his cane, entered the room wearing a black suit over a white T-shirt and a long white scarf. "And it burns, burns, burns," he sang in a low voice. "The heart of fire. The heart of fire."

He paused to pick up his two new kittens, Johnny and Cash, which Haley and Devon had given him as a welcome-home-from-the-hospital gift.

Just then, Irene entered the house solo, ner-vously clutching her big project for Mr. Von, a com-pleted graphic novel called *The Jade Lily*.

"Irene, dear," Mrs. Willkommen said, gliding to Irene's side. Shaun's mother, who was impossibly tall and statuesque, was dressed in a black pencil skirt and turtleneck that accentuated her lithe frame. "There's someone I want you to meet," she added, ushering Irene over to an elderly gentleman with a white goatee. "This is my dear friend Harold Greene, who publishes graphic fiction."

After the introduction, Irene and Harold sat down together. Irene took a deep breath and handed over her book. Mr. Greene appeared fascinated by the narrative and looked closely at each of the penned illustrations, meticulously examining her renderings.

Mr. Von seemed to be enjoying himself squiring

around his date, Mrs. Metzger. Haley's parents, meanwhile, were nowhere to be found.

I hope they don't flake on me, Haley thought, heading to the foyer, where Devon's black-and-white photo series was hanging. Haley stood by Devon's side as a parade of critics and dealers looked the pictures over.

"You can feel the isolation, the abandonment," a man in a tweed blazer said, without making eye contact with either Haley or Devon. "What do you call the series?"

"The Floods," Devon replied, unfazed by all the scrutiny.

Haley admired his poise. He seemed confident and proud of his artwork.

Haley, on the other hand, had begun to fidget as she saw more and more people wandering into the TV room, where her short film was about to be played.

Haley had had a range of options to choose from when cutting together her piece. Since she had opened her new digital video camera on Christmas Day, she had filmed a satire showing each stage of Coco De Clerq's and Whitney Klein's social downfall. She had also shot a melodrama about Joan's attempts to save the planet from polluters, and the effects her crazy work schedule was having on her kids. But after looking at all the choices, Haley had finally decided on showing *Hansel & Gretchen,* a spooky fable she shot in the Palisades a few weeks back. Her old friend from California, Gretchen Waller, had been in town for an audition and had agreed to act as Haley's lead in the saga of a brother and sister who get lost in the woods and taken in by a witch. Rounding out the cast were Mitchell and Gam Polly as the little brother and the witch, respectively.

As the film began to play, Haley nervously paced at the back of the screening room watching people's expressions, particularly those of her parents, who had just arrived. Joan's and Perry's eyes widened when they saw little Mitchell and Gam on-screen. Haley's mom wiped a tear from her eye when Mitchell delivered his first line in a normal tone of voice and cadence. Everyone laughed where they were supposed to and gasped at the appropriate frightening scenes. Haley breathed a huge sigh of relief.

Afterward, Shaun, Irene, Devon and Haley, along with Shaun's and Haley's parents, all went out to dinner at the Golden Dynasty. Shaun, Haley noticed, seemed to have adjusted his eating habits after that stay in the hospital. He ordered vegetable soup, and finished only half of it.

As Joan and Mrs. Willkommen engaged in a discussion of New Jersey landfills over dim sum, Haley developed a newfound respect for her mom's line of work.

Maybe Haley was softening because she finally had a passion of her own—filmmaking. The screening had shown everyone what Perry Miller already knew—that Haley had a gift for cinematic story-telling, rightfully inherited from her dad.

At the end of the night, after the parents had said their goodbyes and told all the kids how proud they were of each of them, Devon and Haley and Shaun and Irene wandered down to the band shell in the park. It was a warm night. Spring was already in the air. They were filled with the satisfaction and relief of having put on a good show, and none of them felt the need to say much of anything.

"Nice night," said Devon.

"Yep," Shaun agreed.

Who knew if anything would come of the meetings with critics and publishers and dealers? It was enough for the four of them to feel good about their work and proud to have had the courage to share it.

Devon put his arm around Haley and stole a quick kiss. She smiled back at him. "I think I'm going to walk Haley home," he said.

"You do that, slick," Shaun said.

As Haley and Devon walked away, she turned to look back at the band shell one last time. And that was how she got to witness Shaun and Irene's first real kiss.

THE END

In Paris, everyone feels as if they're in love.

Sasha, Johnny, Cecily, Drew, Haley and Reese strolled along the Left Bank of the Seine on their first afternoon abroad. Every time Haley blinked, she was amazed to open her eyes and once again find herself in Paris with Reese. It seemed like a dream.

There was a surreal quality to walking along the river at dusk, past the stone bridges, watching the boats float by down below. The silhouettes of budding trees along the Champs-Elysées was an image Haley would not soon forget.

"You didn't tell me how incredible the city was,"

Haley said to Reese as they admired the Parisian architecture in the golden light. Even the modest buildings took on a majestic grandeur.

"I could wander around this city all night," Reese said, with a mischievous look in his eye. He wrapped his arms around Haley's waist and lifted her up into the air, then growled and nibbled at her neck.

As Haley was already discovering, it was pretty hard to keep your hands off each other in Paris.

"Look, there's a table opening up," Sasha announced, pointing up ahead to a sidewalk café.

"That's the equivalent of winning the lottery," Johnny said, putting his arm around Sasha. "Let's grab it."

Sasha's mother was catching up with old friends that night, so the kids were on their own. They sat down at the table, which gave them a prime view of the sunset, and ordered.

"We should hit the Canal St-Martin later," said Reese, who had become their unofficial guide. He was, after all, the only one of the six of them who had actually been to Paris before. He and his family had just gone in the fall. "Johnny and Sasha, I think you'd dig it."

After everyone had eaten what was arguably the best meal of their lives, and after Reese had shown them a few sights, Cecily dragged them all into a building lit with a large neon Disco sign. The room pulsated with techno music. Haley and Reese grabbed a booth and snuggled while their friends hit the dance floor. As the music pumped around them, Haley and Reese made out like bandits. They hadn't even been in Paris for twenty-four hours yet, and it was already the best trip of Haley's life.

THE END

SPRING BREAK IN QUOGUE

There is no convenient time to have an identity crisis.

Haley was surprised by just how quickly she adjusted to the five-star accommodations at the De Clerqs' luxury estate in Quogue. She was given her own sprawling guest room—the coral suite—which was outfitted with a sunken sitting area and a flat-screen television. If she wanted, she could write notes to family and friends on monogrammed stationery while sitting at an antique writing desk near the bay window. There was a paisley-upholstered chaise lounge for afternoon reading. The bathroom was all limestone, and featured a shower with six heads, a whirlpool tub and dual vanity mirrors.

This is bigger than the entire second floor of my house, Haley marveled, wandering around her private suite, which had French doors that opened to her very own terrace right on the beach.

As she unpacked, Haley could already smell tempting aromas wafting in from the kitchen. The De Clerqs always hired a private chef to cook for them when they were in Quogue, since they rarely liked to leave the estate. Upon arrival, Coco had ordered up her favorite meal for them: grilled sea bass with a miso glaze, and frisée salad topped with locally harvested fennel and radishes and doused with the famous "magic" dressing from a gourmet grocery in Southampton.

Haley followed Coco's instructions and freshened up for dinner.

"Movie time!" Whitney said after they had finished nibbling on their meal.

"What are we watching?" Haley asked.

"Your documentary about *moi*," Coco said, plopping down on a couch in the screening room. She pushed a button, and a cabinet opened to reveal a giant movie screen. Whitney produced Haley's digital video camera.

"Where did you get that?" Haley gasped.

"Relax," said Whitney. "I didn't go through *all* your stuff."

Coco plugged Haley's camera into a port in the entertainment system.

"Coco, really," Haley began. "I've only just started editing any of that footage. It's still pretty . . . raw."

"Are you scared I won't like it?" Coco teased, pressing Play. "How could *I* ever look *bad*?"

And right then, Coco's debauched behavior at Richie Huber's house on New Year's Eve came up on the screen. Whitney burst into uncontrollable fits of laughter. Clearly, she found it all *very* entertaining. But then, she wasn't the one projectile-vomiting into Richie's tub.

Coco, on the other hand, couldn't have had a more opposite response. She sat frozen, paralyzed with embarrassment, completely mortified about her uncouth display. Even in the scenes in which she wasn't drunk, Coco came off looking like an angry, bossy, selfish mean girl, who treated her family and friends like dirt and expected the whole world to re-volve around her.

It was as awful a portrait of a human being as Haley had ever seen. She felt horrible for having made it.

Haley realized that for Coco, seeing her image on the big screen like that must have been like staring into a giant mirror. For the first time in her life, Coco was objectively witnessing her actions and seeing their effect on other people.

As she watched a few-second clip of herself knocking down the pyramid of beer cans at Richie's,

Coco winced. She bristled as she "interviewed" Reese Highland and confessed her feelings for him in front of half the school. But the final straw, which made Coco break down in tears, was when she watched herself calling her big sister, Ali, a slut. The camera panned to Ali's face, and all her pain and suffering was completely evident.

Haley stood up, walked over to the camera and pressed the stop button. Coco got up and silently walked out of the room.

"Wow, Haley, you make really good movies," Whitney said.

"Don't you think we should follow her?" Haley asked. "She seems really upset."

Whitney shrugged and led the way out of the screening room, through the den, out the back door and down the pebbled path to the clay tennis courts, which were, of course, tented for spring.

Coco indignantly picked up a racket and flipped on the automatic ball machine. As balls came hurling at her, she smashed one after another across the net.

"Wow, that's a killer forehand," Haley said to Whitney as they just tried to stay out of Coco's way.

"Well, it should be," Whitney said, adding, "she's had eleven years of lessons."

"Then why doesn't she play on Hillsdale's team? Or compete in local tournaments?" Haley asked.

Whitney shrugged again. "I always thought the only reason Coco even took lessons was because she liked the way she looked in those skirts."

As Coco placed shot after power shot with precision at the opposite baseline, and moved from her forehand to backhand with grace and ease, Haley realized that she was watching pure, natural talent, honed by years of training. It was a rare and beautiful thing to see.

Maybe Coco De Clerq wouldn't be transformed overnight, but Haley knew this was a watershed moment in her friend's life. She felt as if she'd just glimpsed the future Coco, and she really liked what she saw.

Haley also felt as if she was partially responsible for the former teen queen becoming a future tennis star. After all, it was her film that acted as the catalyst. Haley Miller was the reason Coco De Clerq was about to change her life.

THE END

SPANISH HOLIDAY

The best thing about
Spain? The siestas.

On the evening Haley, Annie, Dave and Sebastian touched down in Seville, Mr. and Mrs. Bodega were not waiting to pick them up at the airport, as Haley had expected.

"They're in Madrid until tomorrow," Sebastian casually explained, leading his friends out of the airport and into the night.

Haley hesitated. *So we're in Europe with no chaperones,* she realized, wondering what Joan and Perry would think. *Then again, I've basically been living in Hillsdale with no chaperones for months.*

Dave began laughing awkwardly. At first he seemed to be having some kind of nervous fit or spastic attack, but then he announced joyfully, "My mother is thousands of miles away! I'm free! I'm free!"

On the second "free," Dave's voice cracked.

"Oh, brother," Annie moaned, saying to a group of travelers in the airport, "excuse my boyfriend. He's going through delayed puberty."

"What are we going to do?" Haley asked Sebastian in a businesslike tone. "How will we get to your house?"

"Don't worry," Sebastian said. "There are many cabs. And I shall cook for you tonight. My parents will be back in the morning. No problemo."

Haley smiled at Sebastian's playful expression. *No problemo?* she thought, wondering if he'd intentionally booked the flights so that they arrived in Seville a day ahead of his parents.

The cabbie dropped them off at the Bodegas' countryside estate. Sebastian tried to explain how the ancient stone house was situated in the middle of an expanse of hillside vineyards that had been harvested by generations of Bodegas. But it was too dark to see anything. All Haley could see was the stars. There were billions of them.

Once inside the house, Haley dropped her bags and relaxed. It was *perfect*. There were stone floors, and rustic furniture, and a big open kitchen that had a long pine table and an old cast-iron stove.

After Sebastian took them on a tour of the place, he escorted the girls to one of the guest rooms. "Annie and Haley," he said, welcoming them to their modest quarters. "Please, make yourselves at home."

"Where am I staying?" Dave asked, his eyes wide with anticipation.

Dave, as Haley knew, was used to spending nights in a completely sterile environment. His mother sometimes even made him sleep in a bubble. The thought of now going to bed on an old horsehair mattress with no screens on the windows was probably dangerous and riveting for Dave, Haley realized.

Once the boys were gone, Annie piped up. "Can I ask you something?" she said, in a serious tone. Without waiting for a response from Haley, she continued, "Dave and I have never had a, you know, a sleepover before. And I am thinking tonight might be our only chance to be alone on this trip. Would you mind if I—"

"Disappeared for the night?" Haley asked. "Not at all."

Before Haley could even finish her sentence, Annie and her bags were gone. Haley didn't lay eyes on either Dave or Annie again until morning.

Sebastian cooked her a simple vegetarian risotto dinner, using vegetables picked from the garden and locally made cheese. They stayed up late on the back terrace, looking at the constellations while Sebastian told stories about growing up in Seville.

They must have drifted off to sleep on the living

room sofa, because Haley woke up with her head still resting on Sebastian's chest. They were covered by only a thin blanket. A rooster crowed in the back-yard. Haley and Sebastian looked at each other and said simultaneously, "Breakfast?"

While Sebastian made frittatas, Haley folded up the blanket and washed her face.

"Buenos días," Sebastian said conspiratorially when Haley finally joined him in the kitchen. He had already pressed coffee and was now squeezing fresh orange juice. The table on the back patio was set, un-der a big white shade umbrella. Haley stepped out onto the terrace and marveled at the incredible view.

"Sebastian, it's gorgeous," she said, looking out at the rows of grapes, sloping hillsides and scattered buildings stretching down into the valley. In that mo-ment, Haley knew it was going to be a great trip, and that she'd made the right choice for spring break.

Just as Haley and Sebastian sat down to break-fast, Annie and Dave finally emerged from their sleeping quarters, looking like cats that had just eaten two canaries.

The minute Haley laid eyes on them, she knew something was up.

"¡Buenos días," Sebastian boomed.

"Buenos días," Annie replied, acting oddly shy. She turned to Dave and nudged him.

"Buenos días," Dave said in a deep, velvety baritone.

Haley stared at him in amazement. His voice had dropped overnight!

"You must have slept really well, David," Sebastian said with a broad smile.

"Yeah," Haley agreed. "What happened to you two?"

"Can't you tell, Haley?" Sebastian teased. "Dave came to my country to become a man. And he succeeded."

Dave's eyes grew wide, but Annie just shrugged and said "Jet lag" before joining Sebastian and Haley at the table.

Haley didn't know whether or not to believe her friend, but she figured she would have plenty of time to get to the bottom of what had gone on between Annie and Dave. At this point, nothing could diminish her excitement about the nine days they had left in Seville. Nothing at all.

THE END

LIZ RUCKDESCHEL was raised in Hillsdale, New Jersey, where *What If* . . . is set. She graduated from Brown University with a degree in religious studies and worked in set design in the film industry before turning her attention toward writing. Liz currently lives in Los Angeles.

SARA JAMES has been an editor at *Men's Vogue*, has covered the media for *Women's Wear Daily*, has been a special projects producer for *The Charlie Rose Show*, and has written about fashion for *InStyle* magazine. Sara graduated from the University of North Carolina at Chapel Hill with a degree in English literature. She grew up in Cape Hatteras, North Carolina, where her parents have owned a surf shop since 1973.

Haley choose to spend it with? Devon? Or Reese? Or will she keep her options open and keep playing the field?

And what if . . . a boy wants her to go further than she's ready to?

Annie Armstrong and Dave Metzger came back from spring break looking closer than ever. So much so that Haley's starting to wonder what they're doing behind closed doors. Are Hillsdale's resident geeks actually getting physical? And is Haley ready to find out?

With deadlines for the school yearbook approaching, Annie keeps insisting that Haley Miller might have a shot at being named Best All-Around. But will Annie count the ballots accurately? Or is this a rigged election, part of Annie's grand scheme to permanently unseat Coco De Clerq as the most popular girl in the class? Who will end up with the title Best-Looking? Most Likely to Succeed? Class Clown?

Post–spring break, Coco seems to have accepted her recent social demotion, now that she has more important things to worry about. She joins the Hillsdale varsity tennis team and within weeks is regionally ranked.

With Coco now focused on perfecting her game instead of promoting her popularity, Spencer Eton begins to see her in a new light. Will the reformed bad boy and queen bee finally get together as a couple? And is each the key to melting the other's icy heart?

Meanwhile, Sasha is still playing guitar for the Hedon. But with the Battle of the Bands fast approaching, Johnny Lane seems to be treating her more like a bandmate than a girlfriend. Will their musical collaboration cost them their relationship?

Whitney's mom is getting more serious with Sasha's dad. With their parents contemplating cohabitation, will Whitney and Sasha finally reconcile and salvage their lifelong friendship? And now that Coco is spending most mornings and afternoons on the tennis court, what will Whitney do with her newfound free time?

For Hillsdale's most talented artists, love is in the air. Irene and Shaun have finally kissed. But will it transform their friendship into something more? Or make things awkward between them? And how will Haley and Devon cope if their foursome falls apart?

This spring, everyone is doing *something* at Hillsdale High. Annie, Hannah, and Dave are all studying for final exams. Irene, Shaun, and Devon are getting edgy makeovers involving tattoos and piercings. Coco, Whitney, and Sasha are all focused on realizing their dreams. And several couples are considering moving past making out.

The question is, will Haley start "doing it" too? Will she give in to peer pressure—or boy pressure? Or will she have the courage to stand up for herself?

You decide this fall.